RUNNIN' FROM TROUBLE

TROUBLE

AN OREGON TRAIL WESTERN ADVENTURE
THE TANNERS – BOOK 2

William Tresler

Contents

Chapter 1
The Tanners

Noel Tanner clenched his fists. If he could have, he would have planted a solid right jab on Vernon Carlton's hawklike nose. All that held him back was the knowledge the sheriff would believe Vernon's account and not his. He could not afford to spend a night in the county jail with his wife, Dearbhla, and little girl, Fiona, alone on the ranch.

"I ain't got any money right now, Mr. Carlton," he said stiffly, feeling his blood boil. "I sure am fixin' t' pay, but I just can't give ya what I ain't got. If you come back in a—"

"That's been your excuse for nigh on six months, now, sonny," Vernon growled, "and my patience is wearin' mighty thin."

"It ain't like I can talk them crops out of the ground," Noel said between gritted teeth. Everything in him wanted to dislodge his creditor's front teeth. "Nor talk the rain out of the dang sky. I'm good for it, I just—"

"Yeah, I know. You just need time," Vernon cut him short once again. "Well, sonny, time just ran out, so I reckon you come up short. Now, I know you got some valuables in this house. Some of 'em heirlooms from your mammy and pappy, bless their souls." He made the sign of the cross with a self-satisfied smirk on his face.

Noel had to take a deep breath and count slowly to ten to stop himself from lunging at the man. "I ain't sellin' my folks' things," Noel refused.

"Of course, there is another way," Vernon went on as if he hadn't even heard Noel. "This here ranch would easily cover the money you owe me and more. I'll tell ya what: You hand over this place's title deed, and I'll consider your debt paid. Heck, I'll even give ya the extra so you can find someplace else to stay."

"I ain't sellin' my folks' place, neither," Noel insisted stubbornly. Men like Vernon had a way of bringing out the most mule-headed side of him, and he wasn't a pushover at the best of times.

Vernon's face darkened as he stepped closer, his eyes narrowing and glinting maliciously. He grabbed Noel by the front of his shirt. "You better count your words real careful, sonny boy," he snarled. "I ain't askin' ya, I'm tellin' ya. You better hand me that deed and get your sorry behind off this land before you end up in an accident like your folks. This place didn't bring 'em anything good, and it sure as heck won't bring you any either."

Noel felt the blood drain from his face as the import of Vernon's words sank into his brain. They had sounded ominously like a threat. And they sounded horrifyingly like Vernon had had a hand in his parents' deaths. His mind grappled with the how of the idea and could come up with nothing in that moment.

A heart attack while driving the family's buggy? A lingering weakness and eventual passing that looked simply like a broken heart? How could those things possibly have been brought about by an outside force? But it was clear by the look in Vernon's eyes that he meant every word and was sure he could carry out his threat.

"It ain't here," Noel lied. "It's in the bank at Independence."

"Well you better start packing your saddle bags and head on out there to get it, hadn't ya?" Vernon pulled him closer, his leathery face all but touching Noel's.

The younger rancher refused to look away. That would show the man he was intimidated, and he wasn't about to give him that kind of satisfaction. He held the crooked rancher's gaze without flinching.

"Harrumph," Vernon snorted. "You reckon you're a tough customer, don't ya? We'll just see about that."

With that, he shoved Noel away, turned on his heel, and stomped from the ranch house. "You've got till the end of the week," he flung over his shoulder as he rode off.

Noel watched him go, conscious that the few days to the end of the week wasn't much time for him and Dearbhla to decide on a course of action.

She emerged from the kitchen of their humble but spacious house, uncocking the house gun in her hands. "I wonder if the old devil knows how close he came to a bullet through his skull," she said, her face tense.

"You wouldn't have shot him, Dearbhla, I know you. You wouldn't hurt a fly."

"Oh, that may be so, but I swear on the Blarney Stone I *would* hurt a bleedin' eejit who's hurtin' my man," she retorted as Noel took her in his arms. He could feel she was still shaking.

"And you'd regret it afterward," Noel told her gently.

"I know," Dearbhla admitted. Then she looked up into her husband's eyes. "What was he sayin' about your mam and da's accident? Lord love me, but I swear it sounded like he was responsible for it."

Noel sighed and nodded grimly. "Sounded that way t' me, too, buttercup."

"I never thought it would come to this, but what are we to do?" Dearbhla placed the gun on a side table and sat down on the settee beside it. "If I had any faith in the sheriff of this godforsaken place, I'd be knockin' down his door right now."

Noel sat down beside her. "So would I. But I reckon the sheriff's in on it."

"In on what is the question," Dearbhla lamented.

"They want to run us off here." He had known it for some time and naively hoped they would change their minds and move on to bothering folks who had more to give. Now he knew they were going nowhere, and he had to act proactively.

"But why, for heaven's sakes? What've we ever done to any of them?"

"Oh, they don't need a reason." Noel placed an arm around his wife's shoulders. "Though I have been wonderin' if there's somethin' on this land we don't know about that Vernon does."

"Or maybe he's just greedy. Wants to own every square foot of land on this side of the Missouri River." She leaned against Noel and then echoed the question that had flitted through his own mind moments before. "But how on earth could he have caused your folks' deaths? I don't understand it."

Noel felt his gut twist into a knot. Instantly he was back at the day of his father's funeral, watching his mother in her only black dress, her head covered in a black shawl that a neighbor had given her. She had moved like one in a dream, simply staring blankly at people who expressed their sincere condolences in hushed whispers. Vernon had been one of them, and Noel remembered thinking that he seemed rather blasé for a man at a funeral.

While others spoke behind their hands in soft voices and cast frequent sorrowful, sympathetic glances in Noel and his mother's direction, Vernon had strolled about, starting conversations about meat prices and the upcoming harvest time with other ranchers in the room. Noel had brushed it off as just being Vernon's bent to not really care about other people, but now it seemed to hold a far more sinister implication.

Once all the townsfolk had paid their respects and left the ranch, Margie Tanner and Noel had sat on the settee together while Dearbhla put Fiona down for her afternoon nap. "You know that Vernon feller, he's been a superb neighbor," his mother had said, her eyes gazing through the open window to the prairie beyond.

"How's that, Ma?" Noel had asked for no reason other than to keep her talking about cheerful things that could take her mind off the sudden loss of her beloved husband of over two decades.

"Well, you know about the baked goods he and his missus have been sendin' over, and some mighty fine sweets they are. Now he supplies me with some tablets that are good for the constitution. Says now that your pa's gone, I'll need t' keep my strength up." She had pointed to a small glass bottle on the table. It was the deep, nearly translucent blue that chemists used for their wares.

"Well, that sure is kind of him, Ma," Noel had commented, thinking nothing of it, but now he wondered. As his mother had grown weaker and frailer over time, the gifts of baked goods had stopped, and when his mother had died, Vernon had suddenly disappeared from their lives, until the day when Noel approached him for a loan on the advice of the sheriff.

"There was somethin' in those muffins an' sweet breads," he said aloud suddenly. Dearbhla turned to look at him, her eyes wide. "And in the pills he brought Ma," he added, holding her gaze.

"There's no way we can prove that, Noel," his wife said softly, her voice hoarse with horror. He could tell she knew it was true as surely as he did.

"No, there ain't," Noel agreed. His heart ached at the thought of his innocent, cherub-faced little girl being poisoned or whatever other devilish scheme Vernon might come up with. "We've got t' get away from here. I got t' keep you and Fiona out of his claws."

"But where? How? What about you?" Her questions mirrored Noel's own.

He gripped both her hands in his. "I don't know yet, but we'll figure it out, Derv," he assured her earnestly. "We've got to. We've just got to. Start thinkin' about what you'll need to take along for us and Fee if we need t' skedaddle in a hurry."

By the next morning, the young couple had hatched a plan. It was a shaky one, but it was something to go on. They decided they would fill in the blanks as they went along. Noel rode out to Independence to withdraw the bit of emergency money they still had in the bank, making sure some of Vernon's ranch hands got sight of him. If they thought he was going to collect the deed for the ranch, they might think he was giving in to the rancher's demands and relax their guard.

When he reached the city, it was a hive of activity. The streets thronged with people of all colors and in all kinds of dress. There was a blacksmith on just about every corner. Horses, mules, and oxen were lined up in rows, getting shod. Wagons filled the bustling streets, waiting to be loaded by grocers rolling out barrel after barrel of dry goods: flour, rice, cornmeal, coffee, tea, and salt.

"The gold rush still on, eh?" Noel commented to the teller as the man handed over his meager savings.

"That, and the emigrants goin' to Oregon. That time of the year, now. We got us a big wagon train leavin' soon, so I hear," the teller replied, and then looked past Noel. "Next, please!"

Noel stepped away from the counter, deep in thought. He had heard about the land offered by the government in Oregon. Anyone with a wife who had a mind to travel across the Great American Desert and risk their lives facing all kinds of hostiles, disease, weather, and wild animals could stake a claim on 640 acres of farmland that was said to be the garden of Eden.

Why didn't I think about this before? he wondered as he stood on the porch of the bank, looking out over the busy street full of emigrants preparing to leave. A man beside his wagon caught Noel's eye. He was checking off his list of supplies and making sure everything was in order and loaded on a wagon drawn by two powerful oxen, one black and the other brindle.

Noel stepped across the street, deciding the man seemed like someone who knew what he was about. "Beggin' your pardon, mister," he said, "I was wonderin' if you could give me some kind of advice about joinin' the trail to Oregon?" The man looked up from his list, a slight frown creasing his brow. His eyes were a deep, intense blue, and they seemed to pierce right through Noel. He suddenly felt young and stupid.

"First off," the man replied, "if you're thinkin' of goin' this year, you've picked a good time. The fools who insist on leavin' early always end up with starvin' or dead cattle since the grass ain't had time to grow yet. But if you're serious about goin', you'd better get yourself geared up in a hurry. You don't want t' get hit by blizzards in the Blue Mountains. If you get that far."

Noel nodded, his mind spinning. This was their ticket out of Vernon's grip. And a chance to start over. "Thanks, mister," he said, doffing his hat to the man and hurrying over to a nearby smith shop where two men were haggling over the price of the shoes that had just been fitted to a team of oxen.

"Pardon me, fellers," Noel said, butting in on their conversation. The two men turned to stare at him, both of them glowering. "Y'all got any idea where I can get a good wagon and team?"

"If you can pay this crook the price he's askin' for ox shoes, you can have my rig," the smithy's irate customer growled. "I ain't goin' on this godforsaken trail anymore. Reckon I'll just stay here and find me a spread. I heard about too many folks turned around and came right back before they hit the Big Blue."

"I could trade ya, mister," Noel said without thinking. "I got me a spread that I'm fixin' t' sell. House and all. You can keep the furniture too." The man stared at him, looking as surprised as Noel felt at his own words. He wondered if he could take his offer back immediately, but as he watched the man's face crease into a delighted smile, he knew it was already too late.

"It's a done deal, kid!" he exclaimed, grabbing Noel's hand and pumping it rhythmically, grinning all the while. Then he produced a wad of bills and paid the blacksmith with no further quibble. Clapping a hand on Noel's shoulder, he declared magnanimously, "Now, show me where's this ranch of yours."

Noel led him to the only home he had known since birth and showed the man around.

The man had introduced himself as Granville Taylor and was a large, swarthy man with a quick eye and a sharp mind. Once he had perused the house with a bewildered Dearbhla looking on helplessly, he turned to Noel and pulled thoughtfully on his thick, black mustache. "Now, see here, young Noel," he said, his voice gruff but kind. "This here's a good spread. I can see you ain't been successful in farmin', but I reckon I could get something out of this place. I got me a crew of men already lookin' for work, so I'll be pretty much set. But you two youngsters, well, you got a hard road ahead of y'all. I can't bear t' send y'all off with nothin' but an empty wagon, so I'll be payin' ya for the house as well, and everything in it."

He produced the wad of bills again and counted off nearly half. He held them out to Noel, who took them with a slightly trembling hand. He had always dreamed of an adventure, but things were happening too fast, even for him.

"You and your missus and your little un, you make sure you find yourselves a real good wagon train leader, y'hear? With her expectin' and all, you can't afford hitchin' yourselves to a fool," Granville continued to give advice, much like Noel's father might have if he had still been alive.

"I reckon I know just the man," Noel said thoughtfully, remembering the stranger with the two hefty oxen. "But then we'd better be leavin' right away."

"I did like you asked and packed some things already," Dearbhla said, only the draw of her mouth telling Noel she was way more scared than she let on.

"Good," Noel replied, taking her hand and squeezing it. "Let's get that loaded and see what else we can fit in."

"Don't forget you'll still be needin' food supplies," Granville reminded them. "Mind you leave space for those, or you'll starve on the trail."

It was before sunrise the next morning when the little family drove the covered wagon away from the homestead.

Noel sat on the driver's seat alone, while Dearbhla and little Fiona huddled together in the wagon box. He wore his hat low over his face, scanning the hills for watchers but seeing none.

He rode all the way with his heart in his throat, periodically imagining the thunder of hoofbeats behind him, but they made it all the way to the jumping-off spot, as Granville had called it, with no one harassing them. By the time they arrived, the stores were open, and the city was a beehive once more.

With some help from a grocer, and much advice from multiple bystanders, he procured the quantities of the standard staples, as well as some dried apples and peaches. The provisions loaded, he stood on the porch of the general store wondering who he could join up with when he saw the man he had spoken to the previous day standing by his wagon.

Dodging wagons, horses, and people, he darted across the street and held out his hand. "Pardon me, mister, for botherin' you again, but I was wonderin' if you maybe had room in your wagon train for one more family? Name's Noel Tanner."

"You're lucky we're still here," the man replied, giving him a quick up and down glance and apparently recognizing him. "But I reckon you can join us. We ain't as big a group as some I've seen pulling out of here. Name's Landon Morland." He grabbed Noel's hand, and Noel shook his enthusiastically. "Welcome to the wagon train, Noel," Landon went on. "I hope y'all find whatever you're lookin' for out there. I got a feeling we all might run into a lot more than any of us bargained for."

Chapter 2
Recognition

Noel looked around at the fire-lit faces of the families he had come to know and appreciate in the last two months on the trail. For the first time in weeks, they looked relaxed and almost hopeful as the yellow light of the flames reflected in their tired but happy eyes.

Landon, who had ended up being the leader of their wagon train, had hit the nail bang on the head when he said the emigrants would run into more than they bargained for on the trail. Attacks, kidnappers, bolting mules, and giant mosquitoes had been only some trials they had faced together.

But the best part of it was they had pulled together and made it as far as Fort Laramie, without many significant losses. At least, not the crippling kinds of losses some wagon trains had faced. The fort was rife with rumors and stories of horrific tales that the womenfolk made their men swear they would not repeat in the hearing of the children, but it was inevitable they would come to hear them, too.

"You know how Scott's Bluff got its name, don't you, Matt?" Noel heard Billy, the son of Clyde Henderson, Landon's second-in-charge, asking his brother.

"No, I don't," Matt replied, falling right into Billy's trap. Noel noticed their younger sister, Tess, who was sitting nearby, turned her head just enough to better catch Billy's words.

"Rumor has it Hiram Scott was a trapper, many years ago. He was on his way back from an expedition in the Rockies, and he got sick. Probably with the dysentery or something, like some folks in our wagon train did. Well, the leader of the expedition sent him off down the river in a bull boat, with two other fellers to look after him and get him here to Fort Laramie for proper treatment."

Billy looked around to see if he had anyone's attention besides his brother's, and Tess turned her focus to her mother's conversation with Landon's wife, Louise. Billy, satisfied his sister was listening in, continued, his voice taking on the timber of one telling a fearsome tale.

"Only problem was, the two fellers left him stranded on the banks of the North Platte to die. Desperate for help, he crawled and staggered all the way over the bluff, trying to get to the fort. The next spring, they found his skeleton, his bones all white, the flesh eaten away by animals. Or so everyone thinks..."

Tess shivered, and Noel was convinced Billy noticed it too. He smiled and concluded his story.

"Anyhow, since then the bluffs have been called Scott's Bluff, and folks say they can hear his ghost wailing around the infirmary here at the fort, asking for help, but of course it's too late..."

Tess spun around, her eyes wide with fright. "Oh, Billy! That's a lie! I won't believe it!" she cried, her shrill voice and pallid features belying her protestations of fearlessness.

"Suit yourself," Billy replied with a grin and a nonchalant shrug of his shoulders.

"Billy, you know Ma doesn't like you scaring the girls," Matt accosted him in a brotherly manner.

Noel chuckled. If he had had sisters, he probably would have done exactly the same to them. He looked over at Dearbhla, who was deep in conversation with Gyorgyike, the Hungarian mail-order bride of another pilgrim in their group, Connor Slade. Fiona was playing some kind of hopscotch game with Landon's seventeen-year-old daughter, Carrie, a blonde beauty who was almost as tough as her father, and Nellie, Clyde's daughter of sixteen years.

They were all good people, each with their peculiarities, of course, but Noel couldn't help wondering what they would do if they knew he had come on the trail to flee his debt. Of course, he reasoned, he hadn't done anything wrong—the man had threatened their lives, after all—but how many people would believe a story like that? More likely, they would simply make that a reason to distrust him and Dearbhla.

He stared at his wife, even more beautiful than ever, with her distended belly, one hand resting on it as if instinctively protecting the growing child in her womb. There was barely a month and a half left before their second child was due to be born. Noel had already been probing Landon's vast store of knowledge about the trail to get an idea of what they would call the little one. He wanted to name him after a landmark along the trail, hopefully near the place where he was born.

Dearbhla was not as enamored with the idea as he was, but Noel was sure she would come around at some point. She looked up as if she could feel his eyes on her, and he knew that such was most likely the case. Dearbhla seemed to know things other people didn't. She always said it was because she was Irish.

She smiled at him and beckoned him closer. Noel rose and stepped quickly to her side without hesitation. "I'm dyin' for a slice or six of Washington cake again, love," she told him. "Won't you see if there's someone at the bakery, and if they have any?"

"That little feller sure has a sweet tooth," Noel joked, squatting down beside his wife and covering her hand with his.

"What makes you so sure it's a boy?" Dearbhla asked, smiling down at him.

"You ain't the only one can sense things she can't see," he teased. "I'll go wake up that baker if his bakery ain't open. Your wish is my command, my queen." He stood up again and bowed with an exaggerated flourish, making Dearbhla laugh. It was strange, but even though the wagons were still circled in the way they had been all along the trail, with the cattle corralled in the middle and the campfires burning in front of every second or third wagon, he felt giddy with the sense of being close to some kind of civilization.

The irony was that he wasn't sure they were safe, necessarily. All around were camps, one or two other wagon trains like theirs, taking a well-earned rest before they embarked on the second two-month leg of their journey, and there were also smaller camps. Noel could only guess at their reasons for being out in this wild country. Some were most likely trappers. Then there were the forty-niners on their way to California to find the gold in "them thar hills."

There were also Lakota villages. He had been told the formidable gatherings of rawhide lodges were mobile and could pick up and move at almost a moment's notice. Noel had wondered how that was possible with the attending menagerie of children and dogs that seemed to be continually getting under everyone's feet, even while they were camped out and going nowhere.

As he passed one of them on the way to the fort itself, he could see the men dancing around a fire, their rich, dark skin glistening in the light of the flickering flames, their melancholy chants echoing in a strange sort of melodic discordance over the darkened prairie. Somewhere, a wolf howled as if in reply, and Noel was happy to enter the more familiar huddle of buildings that was the white man's fort.

He ducked inside the only fortified part, which had been the original fort before it grew too big to surround with a wall. Now, the long double- and single-story rows of barracks lined a large parade ground, along with the stables, the sutler's store, and the bakery. A large walled compound, which was the only walled part of the fort and was said to have been the original fort building, stood on the south side near the river, while the officer's quarters was housed in a large, imposing structure rather aptly named Old Bedlam.

Here and there, a group of soldiers huddled around a fire, playing card games or just drinking and singing raucous songs to the accompaniment of a fiddle or a banjo. Some men stood smoking and talking, the red hot ends of their pipes or cigars glowing in the semi-gloom. Noel headed straight for the bakery, hesitant to involve himself in any conversations.

Thankfully, the baker was just locking up the building when Noel arrived. He was quite happy to furnish his unexpected customer with some of the desired Washington cake, and Noel gratefully paid him. He was on his way back to his wagon train when a man loomed up out of the darkness and bumped into him. His breath reeked of alcohol and hit Noel almost as hard as the man's shoulder against his chest.

"Watch where you're goin', mister," the man slurred, and Noel couldn't help grinning at the irony.

He stepped aside and was about to move on when the man stopped and looked closely at him in the pale moonlight.

"Say, do… do… do I know you?" he forced his incoherent tongue to form the words.

Noel's first reaction was to deny it, but as he took another step toward his companions, the man staggered into his path, and he got a good look at his features. His stomach contracted at the same time the muscles on his jaw tightened. It couldn't be. What were the chances, out here in the middle of nowhere, that he would run into one of Vernon's ranch hands? Or perhaps ex-ranch hand, since the man was literally hundreds of miles from his place of employment.

"I don't know," Noel lied, looking down. "I reckon not." He made another move to continue on to his destination, but the inebriated ranch hand held him back with an iron grip on his shoulder.

"I… I… th… think I do," the man insisted. "But where…"

Noel didn't let him finish his sentence. "Maybe I just look like someone you know. What do they call it? A doppelgänger, I think," he suggested, remembering something his pa had taught him about drunk men. Provide a quick solution to their question, no matter whether it really was a solution, and they would leave you in peace. Thankfully, it worked this time.

"Ah… ah… yeah, that's it. That's it. Well… whaddaya know?" He nodded, looking as if his head was too heavy for his neck and then he stumbled off on his original mission, leaving Noel gasping for breath, literally and figuratively. He seemed to have narrowly escaped something, but there was no guarantee he would be so lucky again.

Hurrying back to the emigrant's camp, he delivered the Washington cake to an ecstatic Dearbhla and then drew Landon aside. "I know it's irregular and all," he said breathlessly, "but me and Derv, I reckon we'll be leavin' first thing in the mornin'."

Landon gave him a sidelong glance. "You sure about that, cowboy?" There was that unmistakable tone in his voice that told Noel he knew there was more to the statement than was immediately obvious.

"It's the best." Noel was adamant. "I'm sure y'all will catch up with us soon anyhow."

"If somebody else don't beat us to it. Somebody you'd rather not have catchin' up to ya." Landon turned away for a moment and spat out a glob of well-chewed tobacco.

Noel tried to read in his face if he already knew about Vernon and his ranch hand. Before he could answer, though, Landon went on.

"Now, I'll lay off ya if you think it ain't any of my business, but I reckon that little wife of yours is gettin' close to her deliverin' time. Can't say I'd call a man wise who goes off on his own with his wife so near birthin'."

"She's still got more than a month to go," Noel protested. He was feeling antsy. There was no telling where Vernon's ranch hand was, and a man in a drunken stupor was wildly unpredictable. He could already almost see him stumbling into the camp and insisting he recognized Noel.

Worse, what if he ran into him again the next morning? The risks were just too great. He had to get away. He was so consumed with his fearful imaginings that he hardly heard Landon speaking. Then the wagon train leader's words hit home.

"Babies ain't the kind to ask you when they're supposed to pop out into the world. When that little feller shows his face, you're goin' to need someone like Clyde's Anna to take care of her. She's got nurse trainin'."

Noel clenched his fists. There was so much truth in Landon's words, and they were weighing heavily on Noel's mind, but there was a greater fear that overcame all else. Vernon could not be allowed to know where he was. When he had earned enough money, he would pay the man back, simply because that was what his father had always taught him: to pay his dues. But right now was not the time, and he knew Vernon would not wait a day longer. "I've decided," he said brusquely, and was about to turn and leave when Landon's voice stopped him.

"I ain't lettin' you go," he said flatly.

Noel froze and looked at him, dumbfounded. He had thought he had escaped the dictatorial iron thumb of a creditor, only to find his neck was still under some self-important man's boot. "I don't see how you can stop me," he countered, getting ready for a fight.

"You signed our agreement and our rules," Landon said calmly, stuffing another wad of tobacco into his mouth. "In there, it says the leaders of the train may forbid any behavior or action by a member of the party of emigrants that puts another member of the party in danger."

Noel frowned. He didn't understand what the man was getting at, but he was getting hot under the collar. Who did he think he was, telling Noel what to do? What did their leaving have to do with putting anyone else in danger? Quite the opposite. His leaving would *lessen* the risk of trouble for the rest of the wagon train. He opened his mouth to protest, but once more Landon spoke before he could utter a word.

"You'll be puttin' Dearbhla and her unborn child in danger if you leave now. To say nothin' of sweet little Fiona."

Noel felt suddenly ashamed. He sat down on the tongue of the nearest wagon and buried his head in his hands. "I'm runnin' from a creditor," he blurted out. "Tonight, one of the feller's ranch hands bumped into me, drunk as a lord, swore he knew me, but no idea from where. I told him maybe I just look like someone he knows, and he took off, but if he sees me or Dearbhla tomorrow when he's sober, chances ain't good I'll get off that easy again."

Landon chewed a while longer and spat. Then he sat down beside Noel with his elbows on his knees and a fatherly look on his face as he stared at the families sharing life around the remains of their communal supper. "Look at them," he said, nodding in the campfire's direction. "Any of 'em look like they'll let anythin' happen to ya?"

Noel felt a second surge of guilt wash over him. He knew Landon was right. He had experienced a kind of comradeship among his fellow travelers that he had thought was only possible between blood relatives, and then not even all. These people had pulled together and rallied around each other in every kind of hardship they had faced. They had sacrificed for each other, suffered with each other, and rejoiced with each other. "I'll be puttin' y'all in danger. It ain't right," he made one last feeble attempt. "After all you folks have done for us, we can't let our past destroy you along with us."

"It won't." Landon's tone intimated that there would be no point in arguing with him. "You're stayin'. We'll stick by ya."

"Thanks, Landon." Noel felt like crying. More from relief than anything else. The fear of his past catching up with him wasn't entirely snuffed out, but he felt as if he were better equipped to deal with it now that he had the Morlands and Hendersons on his side and in the know.

He sat watching the flames painting Dearbhla's face with a flickering golden glow and listened to her singing a hopeful, longing melody along with a plaintive harmony coaxed from the strings of Clyde's fiddle by its owner's deft fingers.

Now that he thought about it, if there was anyone who could deal with Vernon Carlton better than most, it had to be Landon Morland. Noel fervently hoped he was right. Even more fervently, he hoped his theory would never be put to the test. It would just be better for everyone if that ranch hand never saw him again. What the chances were of that happening, Noel could only guess.

Chapter 3
Life and Death

Dearbhla cradled her belly in her arms as she tried in vain to find a comfortable position on the driver's seat of their wagon. Noel was walking along beside the oxen with Fiona on his shoulders. Through her discomfort, Dearbhla smiled at her daughter's bouncy red curls blowing in the wind.

"Look, Papa!" the little girl cried, pointing at something on the side of the trail. "A mountain of bacon!"

Dearbhla followed the trajectory of her daughter's pointing finger and gave a little gasp. A vast pile of discarded bacon lay putrefying on the side of the trail. It was a nauseating sight, and Dearbhla looked away. But all around her, the sights of waste lay in glaring reality, and she could not escape them.

The wagon train had frequently come across such abandoned possessions of emigrants who had been forced by one of many circumstances to lighten their loads until only the most vital items for survival were left. This spot seemed to be the worst.

A leather-covered writing desk, a trunk full of books, and one full of grand dresses and thick velvet drapes. Piles of soap bars and even dried beans were to be found. Heavy iron stoves and ovens, all kinds of furniture, from dressers to chairs and even a wagon that was in good condition but too big and heavy for the steep inclines.

"Good thing we had t' leave in a hurry," Noel's voice broke in on her musings. "Better to go back one day and see if we can find our heirlooms than leave 'em out here to rot or be taken."

Dearbhla smiled sadly. "I suppose there is always a good purpose in everything, isn't there?" Her question was rhetorical, but she could tell Noel understood.

"I reckon, if a body had a mind to, he could set up a good little home right here and want for nothing," Noel noted, looking around at the castoffs.

He was certainly not wrong. Some had even discarded tools and other things one might have considered useful for eking an existence out in the wilderness. All Dearbhla could imagine was that their previous owners had been foolish or depending on others in their group to furnish such items for use when needed.

She wondered how many tears had been shed over so many of those items that had once been the pride and joy of their owners. She felt grateful, strangely, that she and Noel had been forced to flee their home, leaving them no room to even think of taking along anything other than what was absolutely necessary to keep them alive. Shovel and axe, firearms and ammunition, tin plates and cups, and iron knives and forks. Hardy, practical clothing.

She felt the babe stir in her womb and was filled with a foreboding that he or she was getting ready to face the world. Suddenly, she wished she could hold the baby back, delay the birth somehow. The world was just too hostile at that point in time. If only he or she could wait until they were settled in Oregon. But she knew that was wishful daydreaming.

She shook her head. The wagon train had come to another river crossing, and there seemed to be some kind of commotion. A wagon train that had left a few hours before them from Fort Laramie was already in the process of crossing, and one wagon was stuck fast and tilting dangerously to one side. It was clearly taking in water and threatening to topple over onto its side, dumping all the contents—a family's only means of survival—into the rushing, uncaring waters.

Men were flocking to the aid of the frantic owners, and their lowing, terrified oxen strained against the weight of the waterlogged wagon and the force of the swirling waters that bore down on them relentlessly. Dearbhla rubbed her belly, knowing she would have to clamber down from the wagon and wade across the river soon, and wondered ruefully how many more river crossings she could handle. All at once, it seemed better for the child to be born so that she could hold him or her in her arms rather than waddling across like an oversized penguin.

But the rivers weren't the worst, she was soon to discover. As the miles dragged on, it became clear the pioneers were headed into the Rocky Mountains. The trail was becoming steadily rockier and steeper, as the name of the area it ran through implied. And still, the littering of discarded goods by the wayside did not diminish. In fact, there were some in their own wagon train who had been casting off less indispensable items from their wagons.

One family had even set fire to their abandoned goods, apparently unwilling that any but themselves should make use of what they could no longer afford to carry with them. It was clear there were more people who had reasoned in this way, as Dearbhla saw piles of smoky, charred goods among the unlikely trash that littered the area. It broke her heart to think there might even be someone who could have made use of it. Still, it was not her place to judge the actions of others.

"Whoa!" echoed through the hot, dry air, and the train of wagons came to a shuffling halt. Dearbhla strained her eyes to see what was up ahead.

"We can't take our draft animals up there!" It was one man in their group, Connor Slade. He was a rambunctious fellow and now he made his voice heard. "Why don't we stick to the river? This is too steep!"

Landon, who stood at the base of a looming dome of gray rock, spoke in less strident tones and calmed their comrade down, along with the others who had hurried closer, drawn by the sound of Connor's protestations. Dearbhla could not hear what they were saying, but it was clear Landon was successfully convincing them to brave the apparently difficult ascent.

"Landon says it'll be easier to haul up this stretch here than t' risk gettin' stuck in the bog around the North Platte," Noel explained to her when he returned to their rig. Slowly, the swaying wagons, with their billowing, quivering tops of heavy spun canvas, trundled forward again up the smooth rock dome. As they came closer, Dearbhla saw deep scars carved into the rock, ruts and pockmarks made by the pressure of many an ironclad wheel and hoof.

"How many wagons must've gone by here for them to leave such a mark?" she wondered out loud.

"Makes me speculate on whether there'll even be land left in Oregon by the time we get there," Noel replied between grunts as he pulled on the oxen's lead rope, doing what he could to help them over the rocky bulge in their way.

"Oh, Lord, help us!" Dearbhla laughed. "I don't want to end up like Joseph and Mary being told there's no room!"

Noel almost fell as he laughed with her. "Maybe we should consider goin' down t' California instead," he huffed, scrambling to keep his balance. "If we can strike it lucky there, we'll be free of our troubles much quicker, and no need for acres and acres of land."

"Don't even think about it, Noel Tanner," Dearbhla shot back at him, grabbing hold of Fiona, who was trying to climb from the wagon seat onto the tongue. "I'll have no talk of goldfields, and you know it."

"Yeah, I do," Noel grunted submissively. "It was just a thought, honey, just a thought."

Dearbhla hoped it would stay that way. Something about the forty-niners they had met along the way, and not only the three who had tried to kidnap young Carrie Morland, had left a foul taste in her mouth. Not all of them, but there were many who seemed to be the kinds of people she did not particularly want for neighbors.

There was something about people who wanted to get rich quickly, without the toil and sleepless nights that such things usually took, that made her distrustful of them. They reminded her of Vernon Carlton, who thought nothing of profiting off the loss and despair of others, as long as his pockets were lined and not too much was expected of him.

But these and other thoughts were soon relegated to the back of her mind when they reached what Landon referred to as the Avenue of Rock.

"They sure chose a good name for this place," Noel commented, walking beside their horse while Dearbhla rode to give the oxen an easier time of pulling the wagon over the uneven, rocky ground. A long line of jagged rocks rose up on each side of the trail, looking for all the world like the backbone of some gigantic creature that had come there to die. It made Dearbhla think of all the dead draft animals they had seen along the route, and she pondered how it was a fitting marker for the trail.

The grass was scarcer here, and trees almost nonexistent except for the odd piñon pine. The sandy, rocky wilderness floor was coated with endless clumps of sagebrush. A few far-off, flat-topped, elongated buttes stretched out like lazy dogs along the horizon in all directions, but they may as well have still been on the prairie, with more rocks and less grass. Finally, after seemingly endless hours of jolting along in the heat and dust, they rested at a place with a spring that Landon referred to as Willow Spring.

As Noel helped her down from the wagon, Dearbhla felt dizzy and assailed by an overwhelming thirst.

Her husband apparently noticed something, too. "Are you all right, love?" he inquired with a worried look. "You're white as a sheet."

"I think I'll just lie down in the wagon's shade for a bit," she replied, and then froze as she saw Noel staring at the skirts of her dress. She didn't even need to look down to know what he saw.

"Your water just broke!" Noel informed her needlessly, his eyes wide in his head. "Little feller's in a hurry, ain't he?"

A familiar pain racked her body, making her cry out and grip Noel's arm.

"Anna!" he cried out.

Dearbhla was mostly aware of the contractions pulsing through her, but beyond them, she felt someone prying her fingers loose from Noel's arm and helping her over to the ground below the wagon. A woman's voice called for hot water and sheets, and a horsehair mattress appeared from somewhere, placed carefully in the wagon's shade. She lay down on it, gripping the sides as the contractions pummeled her body.

Fiona's birth had been as violent and sudden as this one, but Dearbhla knew that, no matter how many children she had, she would never get used to it. The pain subsided slightly, and she looked around. Anna was with her, and Louise. Someone had set up an awning against the wagon that shielded her from the rest of the pioneers' view.

"I'm ready," she whispered, feeling the beads of perspiration running a crawling race down her temples.

Louise got in behind her, helping her to sit on her haunches. With the help of gravity, she would have less work to do. Anna placed a thick piece of leather between her teeth, and she bit down on it. Noel's eyes peeped at her from behind the awning, but he was quickly shooed away by her two capable midwives.

Dearbhla set her focus on the child in her womb, who was on his or her hasty way out, and waited for the next wave of contractions. When they came, she heaved, ignoring the searing pain as she bit down on the piece of leather. She could hear herself groaning and screaming, but it felt as if she were outside of her body.

Between, she rested, closing her eyes and focusing on filling her lungs with air and slowly expelling it. Two times, three times, four times, the wave hit her and she rode it valiantly, until a sudden sense of release filled her and Anna cried out, "He's here! He's out!"

Dearbhla fell back into Louise's arms and let herself cry as the wails of a newborn filled her ears. She looked down at her son through her tears. He was tiny but feisty. He seemed not to have any hair at all. And he was red as a pomegranate.

Noel's head appeared at the edge of the awning again. "A boy?" he asked, his eyes shining but fearful.

"Yes, congratulations. Now, get out," Louise accosted him.

He quickly disappeared. Anna tied off the umbilical and washed her friend's son of the blood and mucus, rubbing him dry with one sheet and then wrapping him in another. She handed him to Dearbhla, who reached beyond her pain and fatigue to take the little wailing bundle in her arms.

"Welcome to the world, Tristan Tanner," she whispered, kissing his forehead.

"Tristan *Willow* Tanner," Noel's voice corrected her from the other side of the canvas awning. It was a voice filled with pride and wonder.

Dearbhla smiled. "Tristan *Willow* Tanner," she agreed, still not taking her eyes from the newborn in her arms. It was a better name than she had feared when Noel had first shared with her his harebrained idea of naming their son after the place he was born on the trail. "If I was to guess, I'd say you liked the name of this place and got born here, didn't you, my little shamrock?"

A couple of days later, after she had rested for a while in the company of only the Hendersons and the Slades, Dearbhla felt especially grateful her son had chosen that spot as his gateway into the world. After passing the inviting but perilous waters of Clayton's Slough, which Landon had warned them to make a wide berth around, they came to a veritable graveyard of animal carcasses; mules, oxen, sheep, and horses, none were spared.

It was not the first time they had seen carcasses on the trail. All along the winding wagon tracks, there had been the remains of animals that had clearly not been strong or well enough for the grueling journey. And the frequent graves they encountered, some burial mounds placed right in the path of the wagons to discourage wolves and other scavengers from digging up the remains of the deceased.

What shocked Dearbhla was the amount of carcasses strewn across the countryside. Dotted about the rocky hillsides they lay, small ones and larger ones, all in some stage of decay. There were even a couple of staggering cows on their last legs, and one lying groaning in a ditch as they passed. She remembered Landon's words of little more than a week before, when they had left Fort Laramie.

"Whatever ya do, don't let your animals drink from the pools along the trail," he had warned them. "Beat 'em away if you must, but only let 'em drink from the river."

"Why is that, Mr. Morland?" Billy had asked.

"Those pools are pure poison," Landon had informed him without drama. "Alkali."

"Oh! This place stinks to high heaven!" Helen Morland's shrill cry jolted Dearbhla back to the present.

For once, nobody rolled their eyes at the young girl's lamentations that had been voiced at frequent intervals along the last six hundred odd miles. She covered her nose and mouth with the ends of her shawl, as if trying to filter the stench of rotting carcasses from the air.

"I reckon I agree with Helen for the first time since we left Independence," Noel said, winking at Dearbhla walking beside him with Tristan in her arms.

"It's so smelly, Papa!" Fiona, once more riding in her favorite place, astride her father's shoulders, joined in the comments that were rising all along the train of wagons.

Dearbhla followed Helen's example and covered Tristan's nose and mouth with the edge of the sheet she had him wrapped in. His little face was screwed up, and he fussed a little, as if he didn't like the smell much either.

"Let's hope these awful pools will be done with soon," Dearbhla said, resolutely striding forward, even though her body still ached from the effort of delivering her son. When five o'clock came, however, there was still no end in sight of the poisonous water holes. Although, thankfully, the amount of rotting carcasses had been reduced.

"I reckon folks figured out by now what the reason was for all those dead animals at the beginning," Noel observed. "Whether we're goin' t' find a place to camp for the night, well, that's another question."

"There's no way I'm sleeping tonight with this awful smell," Helen's voice drifted back to them on the breeze.

"And for the second time, she ain't wrong," Noel commented, the humor missing from his voice this time.

Dearbhla was tired. And she was thirsty. She was sure everybody must feel that way. Noel, despite his penchant for always looking on the bright side, was getting increasingly worried. The oxen knew it was time to circle and encamp, and the mules knew it even better. They were heading for the pools of toxic water, made disobedient by their thirst.

She could only look on helplessly, trying to ignore the stench and the heat and shush her fussing little boy while the menfolk cursed and cracked whips, trying to keep their animals away from the deadly water. If they felt like she did, they were scared, so she didn't mind them airing their lungs in front of the womenfolk, given the life-and-death situation they found themselves in.

Suddenly, Landon appeared on the western horizon, silhouetted by the glaring late afternoon sun. "Keep 'em walkin', fellers!" he yelled, his voice full of urgency as much as encouragement. Only two more miles before we hit the Sweetwater! Then they can drink all they please!"

Chapter 4
Independence Rock

With Landon's words ringing in his ears, Noel felt a surge of strength fill his aching body. Hanging doggedly onto the lead rope of his brace of oxen, he cracked the whip around their hindquarters and urged them on in the wagon train leader's direction. The animals lunged to the left, headed for a pool of poisonous water, but Noel's newfound strength hauled them away from the deceptive waters, keeping them on the straight and narrow.

Using the momentum of their desperate longing for water, he drove them onward, pulling them back into line each time they tried to veer off after the alkali pools. The wagon rattled and creaked along behind them, adding its weight to the forward compulsion. And then, suddenly, they were over the rise and both animals raised their head as one creature, sniffing the air, their ears thrust forward, their eyes bright.

Noel caught the scent, too. It was green grass and fresh water. Clean, rain-drenched soil warmed by the prairie sunlight. He could see an enormous dome of what appeared to be sand or rock—he couldn't be sure in the waning daylight—looking like a half-buried potato in the treeless grassland. Beyond the rock, a ribbon of gleaming water wound along, glittering and dark—and irresistible.

He let the lead rope go, and the desperate oxen set off for the river at a trot. "Sweetwater," Noel muttered to himself, looking around to see where Dearbhla and his children were. As he turned, he saw her just cresting the rise behind him, her face radiant as she held Tristan in her arms. He waited for her to catch up to him, and wordlessly, they walked down to the river where the oxen stood up to their knees, drinking deeply even though they were still hooked up to the wagon.

Noel let them drink their fill, scooping up the cool, fresh water in a cup for himself and his family. Fiona laughed with joy and splashed her little hands in the shallows. When they were done drinking, Noel hoisted her up onto one of the oxen and led them away from the riverbank to where some wagons had already formed the usual nighttime circle.

Unyoking the faithful creatures, he let them loose to graze inside the protective circle of wagons, while Fiona ran off to find her friends from the Morland, Henderson, and Slade families with Dearbhla and baby Tristan in her wake. His task completed, Noel felt a thick smog of fatigue set upon him, along with all the aches he had been ignoring in his desperate attempts to keep his oxen from poisoning themselves. Clambering up onto the driver's seat of the wagon, he stared at the blob of rock in the gathering darkness.

Now that he didn't have raging, thirsty oxen and alkali watering holes to distract him, his thoughts wandered to the man at Fort Laramie, Vernon's ranch hand. He could be mistaken, but he seemed to remember the man's name being Fred Johnson. He had always been the one to bring Vernon's demands for payment each month, taking the little they could afford and telling them the boss wouldn't be happy. He had introduced himself only once, the first time he collected on behalf of his employer, and his visits had never included any kind of social interaction.

Although it seemed bizarre, Noel wondered if Vernon had sent Fred Johnson all the way along the Oregon Trail to look for him and bring him back. *But that's surely a little extreme, even for Vernon,* he thought, trying to assure himself it was purely coincidence they had met at the fort. *Even if he sent the feller, likely ol' Fred won't even remember seeing me there, or even that he met someone he thought he recognized, seein' as he was full as a tick.*

He could only hope that such was the case, but as he lay beneath the canopy of the wagon that night, listening to the sounds of the wilderness and his family breathing deeply all around him, he felt a sense of foreboding that he could not shake. As he lay, staring into the darkness, he wished he could have been on watch that night. Then at least he would have had a sensible reason for not sleeping.

In the morning, Landon called the men together. "I reckon you'll all agree we've had us a rough couple of days," he said and waited till the chorus of agreeing nods and grunts was complete. "So we'll camp out here for today. Let the womenfolk do their washing in the river and stock up on their hardtack supplies. Any repairs needed on wagons or harnesses, we can take care of that. Besides, the poor beasts pulling our wagons will surely thank us for a day off."

A smattering of chuckles rose from the little group huddled around their leader before each one showed his agreement. They returned to their families to share the good news with them. Noel fell in step beside Landon and Clyde.

"I've been ponderin' this dome of rock behind us," he said. "Looks mighty out-of-place out here in the middle of nowhere."

"Sure does, doesn't it?" Landon agreed. "This is the rock I told y'all about, Independence Rock. Some folk call it the Great Register of the Desert, though I ain't sure it deserves a high falutin' name like that."

"Independence Rock?" Clyde echoed. "Isn't that where everyone carves their names?"

"That's the one," Landon said. "I've heard folks use many things if they can't carve the rock. Gunpowder, tar, buffalo grease, paint, whatever they can get their mitts on."

"I think I fancy my name on there, too," Noel said impulsively.

"My Billy's been nagging me for weeks to let him carve out our names," Clyde added. "I don't know why, but I thought it would be bigger, the way folks were talking about it back east. Billy wants me to help him find the cave someone at Laramie told him about."

"The day is yours, fellers," Landon said, a little smile in his voice, though his face revealed no emotion. "You're free to do whatever you like with it. Long as you don't expect me to clean up any of your messes."

The men all nodded in agreement, Noel with a wry smile. He hoped those words wouldn't come back to haunt him as he headed for his wagon to give Dearbhla the good news.

"Oh, bless Landon's dear soul!" she exclaimed when he told her they wouldn't be going anywhere that day. He helped her with the washing, feeling mighty awkward as the only man among a gaggle of women and girls. Every female member of the train was taking advantage of the constant flow of fresh water to wash their families' dust-covered, sweat-stained clothing.

Noel knew Dearbhla must still be in pain, though she didn't let on much, so he didn't mind lending a hand, especially since she had their new babe to take care of. Fiona wasn't a problem. She had made friends with the Slade's little boy, Gabor, and they were off playing somewhere.

Fiona had latched onto the little fellow early in the overland journey, and he had slowly relaxed around her, tolerating her presence. At first, Noel had thought Gabor was a deaf-mute, but later realized he simply refused to speak. Fiona had started answering for him when people asked him questions, although they were both only three years old. It was a fascinating dynamic, and both Noel and Dearbhla had been watching the developing friendship with interest.

Once all the washing was hung out to dry, Dearbhla clambered inside the wagon to nurse Tristan and rest under the awning. Noel took the time to check on all the parts of their temporary wheeled home, greasing what needed to be greased, cleaning what needed to be cleaned, and checking if any repairs were necessary. As he crawled out from under the wagon box after making sure the axle would hold another few weeks at least, he looked up to see Anna standing before him.

"Hello, Noel," she greeted him in her confident but respectful way.

"Howdy, Anna," he replied, smiling in welcome. He liked Anna. She was a good friend and support to Dearbhla, and there was something about her, a peace and contentment he couldn't ascribe to any of her outward circumstances. He often wondered what made her different from most of the other members of the wagon train.

"I just wanted to let you and Dearbhla know you're welcome to join us for dinner today. She deserves her rest after Tristan's birth and the trek through the alkali desert right after."

Noel felt a little embarrassed, but very grateful. "Why, that's mighty kind of y'all, Mrs. Henderson," he accepted, giving a little bow from the waist. "Anything we can bring along to the dinner?"

Anna waved off his offer. "No need to bring anything along. Between us and the Morlands and the Slades, we have more than enough for everyone," she assured him with a gentle smile.

Noel knew that was probably an exaggeration, but he also knew it was more a description of their friends' generosity than their available supplies. "I'm sure Derv'll thank ya, and so do I," Noel acknowledged.

"You're both very welcome." Anna smiled and turned away, heading back to her family and her chores.

"Did ya hear that, Derv?" Noel asked his wife, popping his head inside the canvas covering of their wagon.

Dearbhla propped herself up on one elbow where she lay with Tristan sleeping quietly beside her. "Aye, I did," she replied a little blearily. "Anna and her family are so kind. I hardly know if we'll ever be able to pay them back for all they've done for us."

"That's the doggone truth," Noel agreed. He looked at her for a while, wondering how he had ever been so lucky to land a girl like her. "Did you want t' go look at the great rock register or whatever it's called?" he asked, knowing she would probably be tired but feeling like he didn't want to make the momentous visit alone.

"I'd like to, but I think I'd rather just sleep, right now. Chances are I'll regret it later, but that's the chance I'll take." She smiled wanly at him, and Noel knew it was a wise choice she was making.

"Reckon I'll just mosey on out there myself and sign my name for the both of us," he replied, giving her a grin.

"You do that." Dearbhla lay down again, and Noel let her be.

There were two other wagon trains also resting at the place that day, one that had arrived before them and another that had come along a few hours after them. Children ran about, squealing and chasing each other, pointing at names and signatures on the great domed rock. There was a sizeable crowd and even a couple of booths where a few enterprising men offered an engraving service to anyone with a dollar to spare.

They puzzled Noel, wondering where they came from and why they would camp out in the wilderness. His curiosity got the better of him, and he questioned one old, white-whiskered man.

"We're forty-niners, most of us, sonny," he lisped, his leather face creased into a gap-toothed smile. "We ran out of dough, and now we're drifting around on the frontier, scratchin' out a livin' till we can get enough to light out back to the goldfields."

"You didn't strike it rich there?" Noel asked, feeling a little taken aback.

"Rich? Ha! A feller won't get rich out there, sonny boy. But there's always the promise, always she calls us back. That yellow iron is a hard mistress, but once you've had a taste of her, ain't no way you're swearin' off her."

His words sounded mysterious and intriguing to Noel. He wondered if maybe the stories of easy money and thousand-dollar lodes weren't as common as he had been led to believe. Maybe there were those who just didn't know what they were doing and had suffered because of it.

He spent a dollar on getting his name immortalized on the giant rock and do some good for his fellow man. The old miner thanked him and set about chipping away in the spot Noel picked high on a really smooth part of the stone. A half an hour later, Noel was standing and staring at his family's names and the date hewn out in simple block letters when a shadow fell across him. Looking up, Noel squinted into the silhouette of a man outlined by the midday sun.

"Tanner," the man read slowly from the rock face, and the sound of his voice made Noel's blood turn ice cold in his veins.

He recognized it at once. "Fred Johnson," he said, wishing he could be mistaken.

"So you ain't forgotten what you owe Mr. Carlton," Fred drawled, leaning his elbow on one knee as he bent down to scrutinize the names of the family. "Congratulations on your new son," he added in a tone that made the hair on the back of Noel's neck stand on end.

"I ain't forgotten," he said, ignoring the henchman's second comment. "I always said I'm good for it, and I still am. I'll pay when I'm able. Ain't no more I can do."

"Now, see, that's where you got it wrong," Fred corrected him. "Mr. Carlton, he owns you now. You and your missus and both your little babes."

"That ain't what the law says," Noel objected, standing to his feet and backing away slowly. He didn't like the feeling of being alone with the tall, shifty-eyed man peering at the names of his family.

Fred let out an amused grunt. "The law?" he echoed mockingly. "You see all this wilderness? The only law out here is this." He patted the Colt in its holster slung against his hip. "Turns out the long arm of the law ain't long enough to reach out here. Right now, I'm the law, if you're wantin' it straight."

Noel felt his mouth go dry. He knew Fred's words were true, and it twisted his gut into a knot of fear. He kept backing off, but Fred simply ambled along, keeping up with him as he went. Eventually, he turned and began hurrying back to the wagon train. Fred followed as if he were attached to him by an invisible rope.

Landon's words echoed in his mind. *Long as you don't expect me to clean up any of your messes.* He couldn't have Fred following him to the wagon train. He didn't want to bring trouble upon the people who had been so good to him and Dearbhla and their children. Instead, he headed for another wagon train, hoping that, at some point, if he wandered around enough, he could shake Fred, duck back to his own wagon, and hide out until they pulled out the next morning.

With his heart thumping, and keeping Fred in his peripheral vision, he sidled into the first circle of wagons he came across. A group of men were standing about in a loose huddle, seeming to discuss something of importance, but Noel paid no attention to their words. He simply came to a standstill among them, conscious of the line of wagons circled around behind him.

He saw a movement out of the corner of his eye that could only be Fred stepping between two wagons into the camp. Fred stopped abruptly, evidently comprehending Noel was among friends or, at the very least, witnesses. For a few moments, he hovered there, and Noel had to force himself not to look around. Then, as quietly as he had come, he was gone.

Noel waited a few moments longer, not trusting his pursuer in the least. Somebody cleared their throat. Noel noticed the drone of voices around him had grown silent, and only the sound of playing children, gossiping women, and crying babies could be heard. He turned his focus to the men in front of him and realized they were all looking at him, some expectantly, as if waiting for him to reply to a question, others curiously, as if they were wondering if he had taken leave of his senses.

As their faces swam into focus, he also realized Landon and Clyde were among them. They seemed to be the most surprised of all to see him there.

"He's with us," Landon stated, and some men visibly relaxed. "You all right, Noel? You look mighty shook up."

"Uh, yeah, I reckon so," he stammered, taking another look over his shoulder and knowing he was fooling nobody. "You mind if I have a word with you and Clyde?"

Landon gave him a discerning nod and turned to the other men. "If you boys'll excuse us, I reckon we're about done here. Anything else you folks want t' discuss with us, we're more than happy t' stop in again."

"Sure thing, Landon," one of the older men in the group replied. "Looks like you got some shenanigans of your own t' sort out."

The group dispersed, each man back to his wagon and his family, while Landon placed a strong, lean hand on Noel's shoulder. "Spit it out, young feller," he said, not unkindly. "What's eatin' ya?"

Noel searched for the right way to say it but quickly abandoned all pretenses when he remembered Landon already knew his entire history. "It's the feller from Laramie," he stated simply. "He ran into me again, and this time he was sober."

Chapter 5
Missing

The wagon train members rallied around the Tanners with a fierce devotion, the likes of which Noel had never before witnessed. He still felt guilty for adding his personal worries to their collective concerns, but Landon would have none of his protestations.

"All we got is each other," he insisted as he sat beside Noel that night, keeping him company on his self-imposed guard duty. The inky black canopy of the night sky arched high over their heads, liberally strewn with shimmering, twinkling stars. "There ain't a man here who'd like t' be left to the wolves, four-legged or two, so why should we allow that to happen to anyone else among us?"

Noel's gratitude ran deeper than he knew how to express, but he couldn't shake his sense of guilt at being a burden to the men and women he and Dearbhla knew through some truly hard times. They were all suffering together, and he didn't want to make things worse than they needed to be for anyone. Still, there was no doubt in his mind that, without their help, he would be at the mercy of the wolves, as Landon so succinctly put it.

"We'll surely never forget your kindness, Landon," was all he could say further. Mere words could not do justice to the sense of thankfulness and a deep knowledge of how undeserving he was for that same kindness.

In the morning, with the eastern sky barely showing the first tinges of pink, the wagon train moved away from the great dome of Independence Rock. The only sounds were the footfalls of the oxen, the shouts of the men urging them on, and the rattle and creak of the wagons jostling over the trail. Landon had insisted Dearbhla ride in her and Noel's wagon a little way and that Noel ride up front with him.

He sent his boy, Brady, and Henderson's son, Matt to handle the Tanners' wagon. If Fred Johnson was watching the train move out, hopefully he would not notice that Noel was part of it. Noel himself hoped Fred would think he was part of the train he had slipped into when he had been following him.

He felt bad for the men who would have to deal with Johnson shadowing them until he figured out Noel was not with them, but he knew instinctively they were all tough men who could hold their own against the likes of Vernon's henchman.

The further the wagon train traveled from the domed rock, the more he felt himself relax, until he was finally able to enjoy the cool morning air with the warm sun on his back and the sight of the Sweetwater River flowing peacefully along to their right. They were traveling contrary to its flow, and the ground they traveled inclined steadily upward. There was no chance of fanning out across the landscape. Instead, the wagons trundled along in one long line.

"I reckon I'll just go check on Derv," Noel said to Landon, who nodded his silent agreement and went on scanning the country before them with his eagle-sharp eyes.

Dearbhla looked happy to see him. She had just finished nursing Tristan and was eager to climb down from the wagon. "I don't think I've ever had such a jolting ride," she remarked when he enquired after her state as he rode alongside. "I swear the poor babe would drink buttermilk if it was any worse!"

Noel had to laugh. That was one thing he loved most about Dearbhla. She always found something to joke about, even when things seemed to be at their worst. "I'd let ya climb on down, but I think you'll have t' wait till we stop somewhere, maybe only at nooning," Noel cautioned her regretfully. He could only imagine how bone-jarring it must be to travel in the wagon over the stony, uneven ground.

Dearbhla smiled. "Don't fret yourself, love," she reassured him. "I'll fashion a sling for little Tristan, and we'll sit up on the seat in front. It won't be a riverboat glide, but the springs are sure to soften the worst of the jolting."

Noel blew her a kiss. "You're the strongest little woman I know," he complimented her as best he knew how.

Dearbhla waved it off. "Oh, your flattery will get you nowhere," she laughed, blushing slightly. Then she sobered a little. "Have you seen Fiona since we left this morning?"

"Can't say I have," Noel admitted. "I was ridin' up front with Landon most of the way. Last I saw her, she was with Connor's wife and their little feller, Gabor. I'm sure she'll be with them or the Henderson's children."

"All right then, I'll look for her when we stop for nooning." Dearbhla smiled and fashioned the sling she had mentioned from a bedsheet.

Noel nudged his horse's sides and clattered back to the front of the wagon train. Landon was still there, scouting the easiest trail to follow. This time, Clyde was with him.

"Sun's gettin' high," Landon noted, casting a practiced eye at the late morning sky.

"We've done a fair bit of travel, though, haven't we?" Clyde responded hopefully.

"Yeah, we sure have, considerin' we're climbin' most of the time. That rest we took at the dome rock is payin' off. I just hope the others pace themselves and their draft animals." Landon pointed up ahead. "See that rock face up ahead with the split in it? That's Devil's Gate, if I ain't mistaken. We'll have t' swing south of it a ways. No chance we'll get through that with wagons and oxen."

"Devil's Gate," Clyde echoed. "After that, we'll be hitting South Pass, so I've heard."

"You heard right," Landon confirmed. "But we won't be seein' it for more than a week, and that's if all goes well."

"We should noon there, at Devil's Gate," Clyde suggested eagerly. "I'm sure Anna would love to paint it."

Landon nodded. "Don't see a reason we shouldn't."

Excitement was thick in the air when the wagons circled beside the river on a conveniently flat piece of land close to the great towering rock walls that allowed entry only to those on foot or horseback. The river flowed down through the split in the rock and was hidden from sight by rocks and trees.

As the gaggle of children rushed toward the geological anomaly with a handful of protective parents in tow, Noel scanned the group of jostling heads for the telltale flame-red curls belonging to his little girl, but she was nowhere to be seen. A jolt of alarm shot through him.

Quickly, he rode back to the family's wagon, now taking its place in the circle of prairie schooners. It was unlikely Fiona would have passed off the chance to join her playmates in exploring the mysterious canyon, but if she was not feeling well, she might have been held back by Dearbhla.

As he pulled up alongside the wagon and dismounted, Dearbhla was climbing down, assisted by Matt. "Is Fiona with you?" he asked breathlessly.

Dearbhla looked up at him sharply. "Fiona? No," she replied, her eyes already filled with alarm. "Why're you askin'?"

"I didn't see her with the other kids runnin' down to the canyon," he explained. As he spoke, his stomach twisted into a knot of nauseating worry. "Let's not lose our heads, though. She might be with the Slades. I'll check."

Noel stepped quickly over to Connor Slade's wagon. Gyorgyike was readying the family's tin tableware in preparation to join the other families for the midday meal.

"Howdy, Gyorgyike," Noel greeted, trying not to look as flustered as he felt. "Me an' Derv were wonderin' if Fiona was here with you?"

Gyorgyike looked at him quizzically for a moment. "No," she replied in her thick Hungarian accent, "we have not seen the little girl since we left the big rock this morning."

Noel's ears rang, and he felt a little dizzy. "Since this mornin'?" he echoed, the phrase suddenly morphing from the most mundane string of words into a death knell to his horrified ears. "And Gabor?"

"He is off to see the river canyon with the other children," Gyorgyike informed him, her eyes filling with comprehension and deep concern as she spoke. "I am so sorry. I did not think to check if she was with you..." Her voice trailed off.

"No, no, it ain't your fault. We just figured—" Noel broke off, clutching his hair in his hands as the truth dawned on him that his little girl could be anywhere along the trail that stretched a full six miles back to Independence Rock. He turned around, his gaze roving desperately from one wagon to the next. "Has anyone seen Fiona?" he cried out. "Anyone? Please tell me you've seen my little girl!"

Across the backs of the cattle grazing in the middle of the circle of wagons, he caught Dearbhla's eye. Her face was pale with shock as she clung to their baby son. Her eyes were wide with fear and foreboding, begging him to tell her she had misheard him, that the words that had just rung out across the space between them were not real.

Anna appeared suddenly at Dearbhla's side. "Fiona?" she cried out, adding to Noel's plea. "Has anyone seen Fiona?"

One by one, their fellow emigrants stood up from their fires or crawled out from inside or under wagons. Some came in from foraging beyond the circle for berries or buffalo chips. All of them had the same expression on their faces: wide eyed consternation, a little confusion, and a lot of fear. They all seemed to know the little redheaded ray of sunshine was missing. Their eyes full of pity, they gathered around Dearbhla and Noel, who had rushed to his wife's side. She still stood holding Tristan, her face stalwart even as her eyes spoke of horrible fears that were rising in her mind.

"When did you last see her, dear?" Anna asked gently.

"This morning," Dearbhla replied mechanically. "After breakfast, she said she was going to play with the other children. I let her go. I thought she would be all right. She's always been all right." Her eyes filled with tears as her voice broke on the last few words.

"What's the matter, folks?" Landon asked, striding toward the group of concerned emigrants.

"It's Fiona. She's missing," Anna replied simply, sparing Noel and Dearbhla from having to say the words that scared them half to death. "None of us have seen her since this morning. We all thought she was with one of the families other than our own."

"Have you asked the children when last they saw her?" Landon quickly took charge of the situation.

"No," Noel said. "I watched them running out to Devil's Gate just now. That's when I saw she wasn't there."

"Right. Matt, go find out from the other children when last they saw her. The rest of you men, get your horses saddled, we're goin' to look for her," Landon gave commands, and the emigrants followed them immediately.

Noel felt as if he was going to throw up right there. A devastating possibility had just occurred to him. He reached out and grabbed Landon's arm just as the wagon train leader was about to turn away.

Landon stopped and ooked into Noel's eyes. He clearly knew there was something Noel had to say that carried weight.

"Fred Johnson," Noel said simply.

Understanding flooded Landon's grim visage. "No way we can know that for sure, but we'd better keep it in mind," he stated without emotion. "Anna," he turned to look at Clyde's wife, who was still holding Dearbhla in a consoling half embrace. "Do some of that prayin' of yours right about now."

With that, he turned on his heel and strode purposefully to his horse. Noel gave Dearbhla a guilty look. If he had only found some way to pay Vernon. If he had only made sure where Fiona was before riding up front with Landon. If he had only...

But nothing could do anything to help Fiona now. He had to deal with the consequences of his actions. Feeling the tightness of the lump in his throat, he tried not to dwell on the fact that, most likely, his little girl was enduring those consequences more than he was. It was a thought so horrible to think about. He felt as if it might drive him completely insane if he spent more than a second ruminating on it.

Leaving the women and children with only a few men to keep watch over them, and cutting the children's exploration of Devil's Gate short, the rest of the men gathered outside the circle of wagons and discussed their strategy. They were already mounted, each one armed and ready to do what they had to in order to retrieve the little girl who had crept into the hearts of each one of them. It astounded Noel to see how they all carried his burden, as if it was their own little girl who had gone missing.

"We'll ride out two by two," Landon stipulated. "As far as you can, keep within sight of each other, but fan out across the trail. No callin' out unless you're sure you've seen something. We might have a kidnappin' on our hands, and we don't want t' scare off the yellow-livered snake if he took her."

The men nodded solemnly in agreement.

"Noel, you'll come with me," Landon added and rode off, indicating to the younger man to follow. Quietly, the rest of the men paired up and set out, fanning out across the trail as Landon had instructed. To the left and to the right, Noel could see the other riders in the distance, sometimes dipping behind a ridge, but always popping up into view again.

He wondered how far they would have to ride before they found anything. One by one, the fates that might have befallen his precious child rose in his mind, chilling him to the bone. These mountains sheltered not only Vernon's henchman but wolves and bears, trappers and forty-niners, rivers and cliffs, and snakes and animal traps...

Noel shook his head. He could not let those thoughts cloud his mind. He had to hope. In some strange way, it almost seemed as if it would be a relief for her to have been taken by Fred Johnson. The man was not likely to kill her, since he needed her for leverage. Hopefully, he would not make her suffer for her father's sins. He shook his head again, focusing stoically on the surrounding wilderness.

Suddenly, a sound alerted him. He turned to look at Landon riding beside him. The men's eyes locked. There was clearly a good-sized group of people headed their way. The sound of laughing, squealing children carried across to them on the warm air, cutting Noel to the quick. If it could only be his little Fiona he was hearing.

"Stay behind me and don't say a word," Landon instructed as he turned his horse's head in the sound's direction. Noel followed obediently behind, and soon they found the source of the noise. Making their way down between two rock outcrops, they came across a small valley where a group of people were apparently resting in the heat of the day.

There were no lodges erected. They seemed instead to be on the move. Their lodge poles, loaded with huge bundles of supplies and skins, lay near them while their horses grazed on the sweet but scarce mountain grass. Landon reined in his horse, and Noel pulled up alongside him.

"Shoshone," Landon said simply. Noel did not know if that was a good thing or a bad thing. He surveyed the group of peacefully eating people. They appeared to have a communal love for bright colors. Their clothing was mostly white deerskin festooned with multicolored beads embroidered into dizzying zigzag patterns in flaming orange, yellow, and cool blue or sky blue and scarlet cloth dotted with white shells. They all wore large earrings in various shapes and colors, dangling beside two long braids hanging down over their shoulders.

A gaggle of children ran in and out among the reclining adults, laughing and playing some kind of chaotic game of tag. Some were accosted now and then and made to take at least a mouthful of food before they wriggled free and joined back in the game. Noel watched them, thinking how like his little girl they were, when his blood suddenly froze in his veins.

Her ginger hair shining in the sun, curls bouncing, mouth wide open with laughter—it was his little Fiona. She was wearing a deerskin tunic, pale cream with a bright blue swath of beads along the yoke. He stared, openmouthed, and then pointed, unable to utter a word. Landon followed the direction of his index finger and drew in his breath. Then he looked at Noel and nodded, his expression indecipherable.

Noel felt stunned. He could have dealt with Fred stealing his child. At least there was some kind of rhyme or reason behind it, but this was incomprehensible. Why would Shoshone people take his child and somehow convince her to join them? Did they think children were merely trinkets to be taken when the fancy took them?

He drove his heels into his horse's sides, intent on riding into the midst of the camp and plucking his daughter from the rabble of children. He didn't care what they did to him. He didn't think of whether he stood a chance as one man with a revolver and a rifle against an entire tribe of expert bowmen. All he wanted was to get his daughter back safely to her fretting, terrified mother.

Chapter 6
Lost and Found

Before Noel's horse could take two steps forward, Landon grabbed the bridle, effectively bringing him to a sliding halt on the loose gravel.

"No need to go off half-cocked now, boy," Landon said gruffly.

Noel turned to face him, his heart thudding in his chest, his head feeling feverish and confused. "They've got Fiona," Noel protested hotly, uncomprehending Landon's apparent thwarting of his daughter's rescue.

"They sure have, but charging off down the mountain into a Shoshone camp ain't the way to rescue anyone. You want t' rescue her or get her father killed?" Landon's voice was cool and even, his eyes two gray pools of calm pragmatism.

Noel had no response except to bite back his fury and indignation and submit to the older man's leading.

"Like as not, they'll want to trade her for something. Maybe your rifle or your horse," Landon went on, his shrewd eyes surveying the camp. He seemed to search for the leaders of the village, which was difficult, since most of the village were reclining beneath trees and under temporary awnings of animal skins.

All at once, a young boy stopped in his tracks and stared up at them. Then he began yelling something in his own language, his voice high and piercing as he pointed at Noel and Landon up on the mountainside. Immediately, the rest of the village turned their attention to where the boy was pointing, and children began running to their parents, while the women withdrew deeper under cover, and the men sprang to their feet, their faces drawn and wary, their hands reaching for their weapons.

Noel held his breath as Landon slowly lifted his hands, palms facing forward. "Get your hands up," he hissed at Noel and the younger man obliged, trying to stop his appendages from shaking as he lifted them into the air. In an instant, it was clearly brought home to him how close he had come to death only moments before.

Landon shouted something in a dialect foreign to Noel and then made a series of gestures. They reminded Noel of the sign language Landon had used to communicate with an old Oglala Sioux medicine man who had led them to the new road being built at Scott's Bluff. He wondered briefly how far the wagon train would have come if it were not for Landon and his knowledge of the plains and its inhabitants.

But his thoughts were quickly drawn back to the men below when the tension visibly lifted and they huddled together in a hastily assembled conference. Frequent glances were cast in the two white men's direction, but after a few minutes that felt like hours to Noel, they sent one emissary, a tall young man with rather regal bearing and an especially brightly colored outfit.

He rode up to them on a pale horse that had been painted in colors that rivaled those of its rider and drew rein a few feet away. After a quick greeting, the man conversed in sign language with Landon. All Noel could do was look from one to the other, scrutinizing their facial features to find out whether the conversation was progressing positively or negatively.

Now and then, one of them would gesture to the village in the little valley below, and Noel searched for another glimpse of Fiona. He suddenly doubted it was her at all. Tales had been told at Fort Laramie of villages taking in lost children, or even those who had lost their parents in fights between the local plains inhabitants and the advancing wagon trains of white people. For all he knew, the child could be one of those.

According to legend, they adopted those children into the tribe, taking on the language, the culture, and even becoming so attached to their adoptive families that they viewed white people who tried to rescue them with suspicion and fear. It didn't sound all that far-fetched to Noel, especially as the father of a little girl who loved people unequivocally and unreservedly. She would easily get attached to anyone who showed her any sort of kindness.

"All right, it looks like we have us a deal," Landon's voice cut in on Noel's musings. "This young feller is the chief's son. He says they found the little girl with the fire hair wandering down the Sweetwater River, chasing fish and dragonflies. She kept pointing upriver, and they were headed that way anyhow, so they brought her along, hopin' t' find her family."

Noel felt a cold cascade of relief wash over him like pins and needles. "So it is Fiona? They'll give her back to me?" he asked eagerly.

"Not as easy as all that," Landon stated flatly. "Like I warned ya, they'll be wantin' a price for their efforts, and I ain't one to disagree with that."

Noel opened his mouth to protest, but then he remembered why he and his family were out here in the middle of nowhere in the first place, and he snapped it shut again. He nodded. "What are they askin'?"

"First they want us to prove you're her father—" Landon began before Noel cut in.

"How in the blazes do they expect us to do that?" he blasted in frustration.

"If you'll keep your cool, I'll tell ya," Landon countered grimly but still unruffled.

Noel took a deep breath. "Okay, I'm listenin'."

"They'll take us closer to the camp, and you'll call her name. If she answers and calls ya Papa, they'll hand her over, but with a price, like I said." Landon paused, and Noel nodded, keeping his silence this time and waiting for Landon to tell him what that price was. "You'll have t' give them your horse. Saddle and all."

Noel swallowed. He wanted to object. He needed that horse for Dearbhla to ride on when she got tired. He needed it for hunting to get game for them to eat. It was a good horse, a tough horse. He didn't know when he could get another like it. What he knew was that Dearbhla would string him up herself if he refused to trade a horse for his own daughter. Heck, he would string himself up if he did that. "All right," he said, his heart beating fast and his mouth dry. "It's a deal."

Landon communicated his response to the young man and was greeted with a calm nod of the head. The man indicated they should follow him as he turned his horse's head back in the village's direction. When they were a few feet out, he held up his hand, and all three horses came to a standstill. Turning slightly in the saddle, the young man barked a single word.

"He's tellin' ya t' call out," Landon translated.

For a moment, Noel hesitated. What if he was mistaken? What if it wasn't Fiona? If it was her, wouldn't she have run out toward him the moment they had spotted him and Landon on the mountainside? He beat back the questions. It was worth a try. What was the worst they could do? He had complied with all their conditions.

Giving Landon one haunted look, he let his eyes rove across the now quiet valley, the grazing horses, and the sternly watching young warriors. He filled his lungs with the cool mountain air. "Fiona! Are you here somewhere, honey? Mama's missin' ya!" he called out, almost choking on the words.

Almost immediately, a squeal erupted from the shadows of one of the animal skin awnings, and a great commotion broke out. In that instant, the little redhead with the blue-beaded dress burst from the temporary shelter and ran across the meadow. "Papa! Papa!" she squealed, waving her little hands in the air.

Noel almost fell off his horse, his legs feeling like they were about to give way under him as he staggered forward, his arms stretched out toward her racing little figure.

As she leaped into his arms, he felt the tears come. Sweeping her off her feet, he held her close and sobbed unashamedly. In that moment, he didn't care if all the brave men in the world were watching him or how many horses they wanted in return for bringing her with them all the way from Independence Rock. All that mattered was that Fiona was safe with her family, safe with him.

"Papa! Papa!" the squirming bundle in his arms cried out. "Look! My new dress! It's so pretty, Papa! Full of blue beads, see, Papa?"

Noel set her down before she could worm her way out of his arms and go tumbling to the ground with all her wriggling. "That sure is pretty, honey," he agreed, not wanting to dampen her high spirits but eager to leave and get back to Dearbhla. She had to know her little girl was safe.

However, Fiona was not done. She grabbed his hand, pointing back toward the awning she had run from. A young woman stood in front of it, shielding her eyes against the sun. "She's my friend," Fiona informed him. "Haiwee. Her name is Haiwee." Fiona was dragging him toward the woman's shelter, where more children stood huddled around, giggling and staring with big, curious eyes.

A man broke off from the group and moved closer to what Noel could only guess was his family.

He resisted Fiona's tugging on his arm, drawing her back. "Come on, honey, I don't reckon these friendly people want me to bother them," he said, trying to drag her back to where Landon was waiting, still mounted on his horse.

"No! Come! Come see, Papa!" Fiona insisted, leaning hard toward the woman and her family. The man had joined them now and put a protective arm around the woman's shoulders. Noel looked into their faces and realized they were both smiling. The woman said something to the man, and he nodded. The children giggled even more.

Noel was captivated by their faces. They seemed at peace, as if there was nothing chasing them and nothing holding them back. They were open and welcoming, and he felt himself being drawn to them by more than just his daughter's freckled little hand.

As she dragged him to a stop in front of the family, he felt himself unexpectedly inferior. Their lives seemed simple, and yet he felt they had been through more than he could ever imagine, just looking at them. No eyes could hold such empathy and not have seen suffering and loss of their own. He felt humbled, but it was not a bad feeling.

Clasping his hands together, Noel gave a little bow. "Thank you," were the only words he could think to say, probably because they were the only words resounding in his head over and over. The couple smiled and the children's giggling crescendoed again. "Thank you," Noel repeated, this time instinctively patting his chest with one hand and then holding it out to them in an open gesture, palm up.

Haiwee's and her husband's smiles broadened. They nodded, and Haiwee bent down to Fiona, who was looking up at her adoringly and playing with some beads hanging in a tassel from her deerskin dress. Haiwee turned her and pushed her gently in Noel's direction, saying something that Noel guessed meant, "Go." At least, that was what he deduced from her body language and tone of voice.

Haiwee's husband said something to one of the older children, a serene-faced little girl of about ten years old. She disappeared into the shadows for a moment and then reappeared with a bundle wrapped in a buffalo robe. The girl's father took it from her and stepped forward, holding it out to Noel.

Uncertain how to respond, Noel took it, still stammering his heartfelt thanks, and then he realized Landon was at his elbow, leading both of the horses. Wordlessly, the wagon train leader handed Noel the horse's reins. With no hesitation, Noel held them out to the man and his wife, Haiwee.

"Thank you," he said again as he relinquished his only horse and stepped back with the buffalo robe bundle in his hands and Fiona clinging to his brown homespun trousers while Noel kept his eyes locked on the man's eyes. Instead of a savage warrior, he saw a father, a husband who sometimes doubted his own ability to care for his family, a boy who had secretly never grown up. He saw himself.

"We'd better get back to the others," Landon's voice cut into his dreaming. "Best to call off the search before they go too far. And we'll have t' get you and the little one back to Mama before we do that."

"Thank you," Noel heard himself say one last time, his eyes still fixed on the family as Landon hoisted Fiona up onto his own horse and turned away, leading the animal away.

Noel hurried along behind, clutching the gift from Fiona's new friends.

She was twisting round in the saddle, grinning from ear to ear. "Bye bye!" she called, waving excitedly. "Come visit, okay? Come visit me and my mama!"

"Ya'i peweh, koonah-oambi!" Haiwee called after her in reply. Noel could not understand, and Landon didn't translate.

"Ya'i peweh!" Fiona called back, sending the children into greater gales of laughter. It was not the mocking laughter Noel sometimes heard from children, though. There was a simple joy to it. The children, apparently satisfied their lives were not in danger from the strange white men, ran out into the meadow again. Some of them skipped alongside Landon's horse and babbled away to Fiona in their own tongue.

"Ya'i peweh" came up often, and Noel wondered if it was their word for goodbye. Fiona was also repeating it through her giggles aboard Landon's horse, so he joined in, if only for her sake. "Ya'i peweh! Ya'i peweh!"

As they walked up between the rock outcrops they had passed on their way in, the sounds of the playing children grew fainter, and Noel found himself once more anxious to get Fiona home. "Your mama was worried sick for ya, honey," he said to Fiona. "We'd better giddy up and get back there fast as we can."

Just as they reached the trail once more, Arthur Riley and Norman Hastings trotted up to them. "Hey, Landon," Arthur, the older man, called out. "We heard a racket, everything all right?" Then he saw Fiona riding Landon's horse, and his face creased into a huge grin.

"Sure is all right," Noel replied in Landon's stead. "You fellers better go call in the others."

"Yeah," Landon concurred. "We'll meet y'all back at the camp.

When they reached the camp, Dearbhla was waiting and watching anxiously for the return of her husband and her child. As soon as Noel stepped into the camp with Fiona on his hip, still telling him all about her morning with the Shoshone people, she dashed to embrace them both, tears streaming down her face.

There wasn't much time for catching up on what had happened, but the bare minimum was carried over to the rest of the emigrants who gathered around, ecstatic to see their lost member was found. Between explanations, Noel hastily wolfed down a plate of food Louise had kept ready for his and Landon's return. After that, it was time to get ready for at least a few hours' travel before sunset.

"I sure wish we could hole up here one more night, Tanner," Landon said as the wagon train trundled back onto the trail, the wagons falling in behind each other. "We'll be needing t' get around Devil's Gate and onto the long stretch to South Pass soon as we can."

Noel shook his head. "There's no need for 'splainin', sir," he replied. "I couldn't be more grateful for what all you folks sacrificed already. I'd be a downright hard case t' ask for more."

The wagons rumbled onward into the afternoon, with the sun dipping too fast down to the horizon. Noel remembered

Landon telling Clyde Henderson they still had more than a week to go before they reached South Pass. They could afford no unnecessary delays. He resolved that he would do whatever it took to make sure he was never the cause for a hold up again.

The sun was already almost dipping to the horizon when Matt and Brady came riding down the line, calling out the order to pull into single fi e and follow the lead wagon into a circle. It was time to bed down for the night, and Landon had found a suitable spot near the river.

Noel watched the boys ride by and leaned on his team's lead rope to bring them into line. Suddenly, a scream, a shout, and the neigh of a terrified horse filled the air. Noel couldn't stop and look immediately, but as soon as he could bring his team to a standstill, he ran over to where the sound had come from.

Matt and Brady were already there, kneeling down in the dirt, looking closely at the still form of a man lying in a crumpled heap on the ground. The sound of hoofbeats fading into the distance drew Noel's eye to a horse galloping off into the distance. Tilly Southey stood still with her hands over her mouth as Brady, who had had his ear to her husband's face, stood to his feet.

"Matt, you stay here with Mrs. Southey and the kids. I'm goin' after that horse." He turned to mount up and saw Noel approach in that moment.

"Mr. Tanner," he said, his voice carrying more gravity than a boy of nineteen's should. "Could ya go tell my pa Mr. Southey's had an accident?"

Chapter 7
Wildfire

It was a somber dinner meal in the camp with the gathering darkness descending on the emigrants. A mound of rocks lay off to one side outside the circle, the biggest inscribed with the words, "Benedict Octavius Southey, 1801–1850."

The four families around their communal fire ate mostly in silence until Billy Henderson piped up, "I know y'all don't want t' talk about it, but what really happened to Mr. Southey, Matt?"

Dearbhla looked up at Noel. She knew. He had told her as soon as he and Matt and Brady had followed the Southey's wagon into the circle, accompanied by a weeping Tilly Southey and three wide-eyed, frightened children.

"It was a rattler, Billy," Brady informed him when Matt didn't reply for a moment of thick silence.

"He got bit?" Billy prodded him for more information.

"No, the rattler spooked his horse, and he got thrown. Broke his neck. It was quick." Brady spoke in clipped sentences, as if he didn't want to dwell on the subject too long.

"So he didn't suffer?" Billy insisted on knowing more.

"Well, we can't know that for sure, half-pint," Landon took over from Brady, "but, yeah, I reckon if he suffered, it wasn't for long."

Billy seemed satisfied with that reply and bit down on his share of dried buffalo meat before chewing ruminatively. Dearbhla remembered Fiona had referred to it as pemmican since her brief visit with her Shoshone friends. She had also insisted the pioneers should make it the way the Shoshone did, minced and mixed with fat and berries. Dearbhla made a mental note to try that the next time the men killed fresh meat.

In the morning, the wagon train moved out with the same sense of somber stillness. They had had many brushes with death and heard of others who had come to an untimely end, but it was the first time someone within their own ranks had been physically taken away from them by the inhospitable surroundings.

"The picnic sure is over, ain't it?" Noel remarked to his wife softly while they walked beside their wagon, watching Fiona flit from one patch of grass to another, looking for insects to ogle.

Dearbhla smiled at him. "I've been thinking myself how I only saw the beauty and not the danger. But even the danger has a kind of beauty, doesn't it?"

"I'll wager poor Tilly Southey won't agree with ya," Noel countered, casting a glance back at the Southey wagon. The children had been so shaken up by the incident that they were too afraid to ride the horse in case it threw one of them, too. Instead, they opted to tie the animal behind the wagon while they walked beside the wagon.

By the third day after the accident, Mrs. Southey had composed herself sufficiently to converse with the other emigrants, and during nooning, she stepped over to the Tanner wagon as Dearbhla was washing up her children to prepare for the noon meal.

"Mrs. Tanner," she said, her voice soft and tremulous. "I know you've been poorly since birthing your lovely little boy, and I know your husband had to barter your only horse to get your little girl back. I've been watching you walking alongside your wagon these past three days."

She paused after the rush of almost whispered words and took a deep breath. Dearbhla waited for her to continue, sensing she was not done and there was something momentous she wanted to say.

"I hope you won't take it as an affront, but I can't bear to look at this horse of ours, let alone ride it or set one of my babes upon it. I know it's silly. I know it's not the horse that... killed Ned, but there's no tellin' my heart that."

She paused again while she glanced down for a moment, fiddling with her apron. Then, all at once, she looked up into Dearbhla's face, her eyes wide and sincere and full of sadness. "Jasper's really a good horse. Part mustang, part Quarter Horse. Gentle as a lamb with the children and strong as an ox. I want you t' have him. You need him more than we do."

Dearbhla's heart broke. She couldn't possibly accept such a gift after what Tilly Southey had been through, and yet she also knew she couldn't possibly refuse it. Thinking no more about her response, she wrapped her arms around the older woman and gave her a warm embrace. Tears stung her eyes as she whispered, "I know what this means to you. Thank you, Tilly."

She felt the widow's nod of acknowledgment against her shoulder, and they stood like that for a few moments longer.

Then Dearbhla drew back, looking intently into Tilly's eyes. "If you ever need him, for anything, or if you need to take him back, he's all yours," she assured the bereaved woman.

Tilly merely nodded, her eyes filling with tears, before she turned and hurried off.

When Dearbhla and Noel returned from their meal, ready to prepare for the second half of the day's journey, they found a saddled and bridled Jasper tied to the back of their wagon, looking as if he belonged already. As Noel helped her aboard the beautiful liver chestnut horse, Dearbhla hoped Tilly would take her counter offer seriously.

The wagon train continued along the Sweetwater River for the next five days, days that seemed to melt into one long day of monotonous plodding and jolting along. It forced the men to range a little further than usual with the cattle and oxen, since acres and acres of sagebrush and sand had replaced the prairie grasses.

Each night, they encamped as close to the river as possible, and the frequent drenching rain they had experienced on the plains now gave way to wild thunderstorms with more lighting and thunder than rain. Between the storms, the days were hot, like the inside of a furnace. Energy levels among the pioneers dropped lower than they had been yet, and with them went the easy amicability that had prevailed for most of the journey.

Tempers were frayed, patience wore thin, and Dearbhla sensed a rift slowly forming in the group. Then, one afternoon, a storm passed through without a drop of rain. The massive thunderheads towering into the wide open sky seemed to mock them as they held back their bounty of water and battered the straggling emigrants with hot gusts of wind that filled every nook and cranny with powdery dust.

Bolts of lightning seared the sky, crackling with their vivid white displays of power and filling the air with the booming rumble that seemed to come from everywhere at once. The animals were nervous, and for good reason. Even the men cast constant anxious looks to the heavens, as if they expected to be struck down at any moment by a white hot bolt of light.

As the grumbling mass of cloud passed slowly over them, they relaxed, but then a cry from the tail-end wagon arrested everyone's attention. Dearbhla turned in the saddle, peering behind her and trying to decipher what Norman Hastings was trying to say.

"What is it, Derv?" Noel asked, squinting up at her into the brightness of the hazy afternoon sky.

"I'm not sure…" Dearbhla began, and then she stopped short.

The blustering south easterly that had come in the storm's wake turned more west for just a moment and carried Norman's words to her clearly, but by that time she had no need of them. Her staring eyes told her more than she needed to know.

Billows of thick, brown smoke were rising into the air behind the last few wagons. At their base, she could just make out the glow of leaping yellow flames being driven before the wind.

"Fire! Fire!" Dearbhla took up the cry. Noel gaped at her for a moment and then cupped his hands around his mouth, bellowing in unison with his wife, "Fire! Fire!"

Within minutes, Landon came galloping up along the line of wagons to see what was happening. His eyes grew somber and tense but, as always, Dearbhla could see his mind working behind them, efficient as clockwork.

"Turn right! Head for the river," he ordered as he thundered back past them to the front of the train.

"Head for the river!" a staggered chorus of voices took up the cry. Bewildered oxen were hauled from the already well-beaten track and forced to cross the uneven desert ground. Children ran ahead, trying to move small boulders out of the way or steer their draft animals away from a treacherous ditch in their path. By now, they could hear the crackling of burning sagebrush, and the acrid stench of smoke stung their nostrils, egging them on to even more frantic efforts.

One team of mules, pulling the wagon of a man name Marvin Peters, became so terrified by the smoke and fire, they kicked their traces to smithereens and took off on their own, leaving their horrified owner frantically attempting to haul the heavy vehicle to the safety of the cool waters of the river.

Dearbhla slid down from Jasper's back, still clutching Tristan against her chest. She hoisted Fiona down with one hand and yelled to Noel, "Take Jasper and get men to help Marvin get his wagon to the river! I'll take the oxen!"

He gave her one look and responded instantaneously. Without even watching him ride away, Dearbhla grabbed hold of the oxen's lead rope and forged on through the rough terrain. "Dear God, if you're there, please let us all make it," she begged, her lungs burning with smoke, her hand clinging to a squealing, frightened Fiona while Tristan fussed and keened in her neck, held against her chest by the hammock-like sling she had fashioned for him.

By the time she reached the banks of the Sweetwater, the smoke was almost suffocating, and she could feel the singeing heat of the fire in the gusts of ash- and soot-laden winds that pummeled them relentlessly. Wading into the shallows and dragging the oxen in with her, she made sure the wagon was in with all four wheels before dipping her apron in the water and covering Fiona's nose and mouth. She did the same with her handkerchief for Tristan and took the other corner of her apron for herself.

Standing knee deep in the water, she turned to look behind her. The men of the train had rallied behind Marvin and his wagon, shoving and hauling and yelling and dodging the great iron wheels as they all but carried the heavy wagon across the rocky desert floor. The fire was roaring behind them, now, reaching out with greedily licking tongues of flame, hungry to devour the entire livelihood of the Peters family.

Dearbhla could only imagine how quickly the dry wood would catch alight and everything would be lost: flour, beans, corn, coffee, tea, clothing, bedding—in short, everything they owned on the earth. Her stomach twisted into a knot of fear. *Please, please, please...* the words spun round and round in her head as she watched helplessly, her arms protectively covering her sniffling, coughing children.

Their bodies straining against the weight of the wagon, the men hauled it into the river in time, but not without a few injuries. Some rejoined their own families while Brady and Matt mounted up and went after the Peters' runaway mules, which someone had seen galloping away across the river in a northerly direction. Dearbhla couldn't find it in her heart to blame any creature for fleeing blindly from such an inferno.

Even now, the river was full of creatures: snakes, rats, desert cottontails, ground squirrels, even a pair of mule deer and a coyote, their eyes wild with terror. The animals swam and splashed past, downstream from Dearbhla, where she stood beside the wagon. The heat from the fire was almost unbearable, and she began soaking herself and the children with water.

After carefully laying Tristan in the wagon, she fetched the bucket hanging at the back and began tossing water over the canopy, dousing the whole thing before it could heat enough to catch fire. Noe rode up and dismounted, standing beside her in the water.

It could not have been more than five minutes that the fire raged at the edge of the water, but Dearbhla knew the scene would be imprinted on her memory from that moment on. Noel put an arm around her while they watched the fire burn itself out.

"Imagine if we hadn't been near a river," Noel postulated thoughtfully.

"I'd rather not," Dearbhla replied as she laid her head against his shoulder and wondered how many others had been caught in a wildfire and not been as fortunate as they had.

Once Matt and Brady had brought the escaped mules back to their furious owner and Clyde Henderson, the resident carpenter of the wagon train, had made what repairs he could to the shattered traces, the group deliberated on their situation. It was quickly decided that, since nobody knew how long it would take for the scorched earth to cool enough for oxen and horses and people to walk on it without roasting their feet, the party would stop for the night right where they were.

Struggling across to the other side of the river, they found a reasonable area to camp in and settled down for the night. But that wasn't the only bit of excitement for the journey. The next morning, as the emigrants were getting ready to cross the river and rejoin the main trail, a shot rang out in terrifying proximity to the camp.

Mothers instinctively shielded their children with their bodies. Men reached for their own weapons, wildly glaring around to see where the threat was coming from, but only an eerie stillness hung in the air.

Then a scream tore the early morning silence. "Noooo! No! Harold!"

Harold Jones, a bumbling, loud-mouthed city boy with a slipshod approach to life, lay groaning on the ground behind his wagon. Noel told Dearbhla, afterward, the man had spotted a wolf while making sure everything was tied down properly to his wagon. Determined to have a wolf pelt for his new house in Willamette Valley, he had reached into the side of the wagon and pulled out his rifle by the barrel.

As he had dragged it from the wagon, the trigger had snagged on something and the gun went off, shooting him full in the chest. He lasted only long enough to tell the story. The wolf was nowhere to be seen.

Another man down, and deeply sobered by how quickly the wildfire had borne down upon them the previous day, the overlanders spent the next few days traveling in almost complete silence. Even the children were quieter. There were now two mounds of rocks left in their wake, and it had become clear nobody was exempt. Anything could happen to anyone in the blink of an eye, and there was nothing they could do to stop it.

By the afternoon of the eighth day of travel since leaving Independence Rock, Landon came riding along the line of wagons fanned out across the wilderness to avoid traveling in each other's dust.

"We've reached South Pass!" he shouted with a semblance of excitement, pointing down the trail.

Dearbhla peered in the direction he indicated, trying to find some kind of landmark that looked something like a pass, or at least the image of a pass she had in her mind. All she could see for miles around, though, was the same rocky, unforgiving wilderness.

"How do you know?" she asked Landon from Jasper's back.

"Feller carved it on a rock beside the trail," Landon informed her before continuing on along the wagon train, proclaiming the good news.

"Feels like a bit of a letdown, don't it?" Noel observed. "After all that sameness, I was sort of expectin' somethin' with a little more biggety, you know what I mean?"

Dearbhla laughed dryly. "I sure do," she agreed. "Maybe a little sameness is just what we need."

"You ain't wrong," Noel conceded. "Folks are all tuckered out, that's plain t' see."

Still, that evening when the wagons had all passed the crudely engraved marker that told them they had reached the place they would cross the Great Divide, a certain amount of relief seemed clear in the group, if not outright, extravagant joy. Noel took out his banjo, and Clyde followed suit with his fiddle.

Dearbhla handed baby Tristan to Anna and stood to her feet. She had to dance, even if it was just a little, not the bouncing, rhythmic Irish dance she was used to, and she had to sing, even if only to feel normalcy again before she surrendered herself to the endless miles of scrubland and dust and blazing sun.

Closing her eyes, she sang a song filled with the longing for imminent victory that still seemed so far out of reach.

And if, when all a vigil keep,
The West's asleep! The West's asleep!
Alas! And well may Erin weep
That Connacht lies in slumber deep.
But, hark! A voice like thunder spake,
The West's awake! The West's awake!
Sing, oh! Hurrah! Let England quake,
We'll watch till death for Erin's sake

As the final strains of the song rose up to the star-studded sky, Dearbhla opened her eyes and gazed into the night beyond the circle of wagons. For a moment, she thought she saw something moving just beyond the light cast by the fire, but she couldn't be sure. Deciding to say nothing, she called for another song and turned her thoughts to things that would not bring fear or worry to her mind.

Chapter 8
Dissent

Two days of thankfully uneventful travel later, the pioneers reached the end of South Pass, indicated by the twin buttes pointed out by Landon.

"They call them the Oregon Buttes," he informed his barely interested audience when they had circled the wagons to make camp at the end of the second day.

"Does this mean we're halfway there, Mr. Morland?" Billy enquired, once more the only one of the party willing to speak at the four families' silent supper.

"It does, half-pint," Landon said. "But we've got some pretty rough terrain comin' up, so I hope none of y'all are thinkin' it'll be all downhill from here on out."

He got a few wry smiles for his valiant attempt at humor, but Noel wasn't feeling well enough to be one of them. His head was throbbing, and his skin felt like it was burning, although the wildfire was far behind them. His stomach seemed to be upset, too, though that was not too much of a strange thing. The water along the trail had not always been the freshest or cleanest, and he had grown accustomed to fairly regular bouts of bowel discomfort.

"I reckon I'll hit the sack early tonight, if you folks don't mind," he said, doffing his hat to the faces lining the fire pit.

"Not at all," Connor agreed. "I'm feeling a little feverish, so I think I'll follow your lead."

"Yeah, me too," Matt chipped in.

Landon looked up warily. "Anyone else feelin' under the weather?" he asked in his dry way.

"I reckon I'm just tired," Brady responded, giving an enormous yawn as proof of his statement and quickly covering his mouth when he saw his mother's disapproving look.

By morning, though, it became apparent that tiredness was the least of their worries. From all around the encampment, groans sounded in the still morning air. One by one, they emerged from their makeshift sleeping quarters. Some held their stomachs and dashed off to a rock pile downwind from the camp. Others lost their dinner a few steps away from the camp. All who were sick were running fevers, and some had some kind of skin rash dotting their bodies with rose-colored little spots.

Landon, the picture of health, if a little more gaunt than he had been when they left Independence, pressed his hands down on his thighs where he sat beside the breakfast fire, conspicuously devoid of human presence. Noel watched him from under the wagon where he lay, wishing he could reach inside his head and remove his brain, as it was aching so badly.

"Well, there ain't a snowball's chance in hell we'll be leavin' today," Landon said grimly to whoever was listening.

In fact, it was a full week before anyone was well enough to move. Landon called a meeting one night to discuss the way forward with the rest of the fathers of families.

"I know y'all are pretty tuckered out," he said, "but time ain't on our side. We'd best be goin' but we can't sit around here much longer. All in favor of movin' on, say, aye."

"Aye," Noel agreed, together with a chorus from Connor, Clyde, Norman, and a few more families. Only two were silent.

"James? Harvey?" Landon asked at their silence.

"I don't know as we're doin' the right thing by pushing through this," Harvey said, shaking his head. "We got two dead, almost got caught in a runaway fire, been hit hard by this mountain fever thing, and now we're a week behind schedule. Seems like a lot of signs to me."

"We can still make it," Landon stated simply. "But I won't force anyone who ain't feelin' happy about keepin' on." He leaned back, folding his arms across his chest and glancing from face to face in his customary unflinching, inexpressive way.

"Me an' my folks, we'll be stayin'," James spoke for himself. "Maybe later we'll head on down t' California. At least it ain't as cold as the Blue Mountains."

California. The word still held a brief glimmer of magic for Noel. There were stories of lives being turned around to where previously dirt-poor men were buying their own vast ranches, stocking them with cattle, and building huge mansions for their families or opening successful, well-funded businesses in the city of Los Angeles. He dragged his focus back to the meeting at hand.

"But, like I said, I ain't here t' tell ya what t' do with your own family." Landon sounded like he was concluding the discussion. "We'll be pullin' out in the mornin', usual time.

Y'all are welcome t' join us, and you're welcome t' choose your own way."

The next morning, the camp was a flurry of activity. Some of those who had been sick were still too weak to walk alongside their wagons. As had been the case when they reached the first steep ascents of the Rocky Mountains, all unnecessary items were thrown by the wayside to make the wagons lighter. The already exhausted oxen and mules were now going to have more weight added to their burdens.

The two men who had opted to stay didn't even poke their heads out of their wagons as the rest of the party rumbled away. Down from thirteen to eleven wagons, the pioneers soldiered on.

It was slow going, but the miles dragged by one by one. The stronger members of the train shouldered their extra burdens valiantly, and not one commented on the strain. Noel had been only lightly affected by the fever, for some unknown reason he was immensely thankful for. When the train set off again, he was at Landon's side, following his every instruction.

But not everybody was as loyal and diligent as Noel, as he was soon to find out. One evening he went out to "see a man about a horse," as he always said, when the sound of men talking in agitated tones reached his ears. He paused, listening intently, aware he was eavesdropping but not feeling too guilty about it. If men were going to have a conversation in such loud and clear tones just beyond the camp, they evidently had nothing to hide.

"I asked Landon about Sublette Cutoff again today," one voice said, already sounding sour.

"Yeah?" the other prodded. "What'd he say?"

"The usual balderdash about water and safety and grazing," the sour voice retorted irritably.

"Figures," the other voice replied.

"Thing is," the first voice interrupted hotly, "he's holdin' himself Mr. High an' Mighty around here, but he ain't got a say in what we decide, you know?"

"He don't?" the other voice echoed Noel's feelings of incredulity at this claim.

"Out here, it's each man for himself. If we all had t' rely on some other feller to make our decisions for us, where would we be?"

"Heck, I don't know. Landon's made some pretty good calls along this trail so far. I'd be inclined t' trust him."

"Yeah, but this time he's missin' it," the sour voice insisted. "We're a week behind now. More, if ya factor in the miles we're losin' travelin' so slow right now. We're on a knife edge. Only way we can be sure t' miss the early snows in the Blue Mountains is t' take the cutoff."

"Did you tell him so?"

"Sure I did. Stubborn mule-headed gump won't listen. Says it's been a dry year, there ain't much chance of early snows, and he'd rather not risk killin' the cattle on a trail with no grazin'."

"Makes sense, I reckon."

"Whose side are you on, Jack?" the sour voice was becoming increasingly agitated.

"I just want t' get there in one piece and be strong enough t' do somethin' with my parcel of land."

"So do I, Jack, so do I. But none of us is goin' t' do any of those things if we're turned into human icicles by a Blue Mountain blizzard!"

The men moved away, unknowingly leaving Noel to ponder their conversation. He wasn't sure who the man with the sour voice was, but it sounded a lot like Marvin Peters to him. Completing his original mission, he returned to camp, wondering if he should inform Landon and Clyde of what he had overheard.

It could bring him further into their confidence, but he also reasoned it might easily just be fatigue making the sour-voiced man more ornery than usual. He didn't want to fan a spark into a flame. If something was going to erupt in the camp, it would not be Noel Tanner who started it. He had promised himself that much already.

"Stay out of trouble, that's all I got t' do," he muttered to himself. "Let Jack and his ornery friend cause their own trouble if they've a mind to."

Three days more of achingly slow travel and they reached the point where the split in the trail, leading toward the Sublette Cutoff, appeared ahead on the horizon. It was at a nooning just before they reached the cutoff that Marvin Peters made his move.

Getting up from where he had sat for his midday meal, he strode to the middle of the circle, not looking right or left. Taking up the pose of one who had an immensely important announcement to make, he cleared his throat before he spoke in well-projected tones, slowly articulated, as if to make sure nobody was left in doubt about what he had to say.

"That over there," he said, indicating the western horizon with one hand, "is what folks call the Sublette Cutoff. It ain't called a cutoff for nothin', either." He paused for effect and went on staring at the far horizon. "If we take that cutoff, we'll practically shave seventy miles off the distance we have t' travel to the land of promise."

Noel could hear Landon groan beside him, but he showed no emotion in his face. The men and women seated around their lunchtime fires began looking at each other in confusion.

"Yeah, I know. Our brave leader, Mr. Morland there, well, he ain't told us a thing about that cutoff, and I'm just as puzzled as you folks are about why he would keep such a fact from the rest of us." Marvin's voice had developed a bit of a sarcastic edge to it.

Landon sighed quietly, leaving Noel with the sense that being a leader wasn't as glamorous as it was cracked up to be. A hum of murmuring broke out among the listening emigrants, to the obvious satisfaction of Marvin Peters, whose chest puffed out like a rooster on a haystack.

"I propose we take this cutoff and save ourselves freezing to death in the Blue Mountains before we ever make it to Willamette Valley," he concluded with great aplomb.

Landon rose wearily to his feet and loped over to the place where Marvin stood. It was clear he was only doing so because he knew there was an expectation for him to explain himself, not because he felt he needed to. Noel watched the interaction with interest.

"Now, folks, Mr. Peters ain't wrong. The Sublette Cutoff truly hacks a good seventy miles off the trail," he began.

"Then I say we take it!" a voice cried out.

"Me too!" another added.

Landon held up his hand. "What Mr. Peters forgot t' tell ya is that there's precious little water and grazin' along that way, and bein' a dry year, as it is—"

Once again, he was interrupted. "A dry year, a dry year," Marvin aped him mockingly. "That's all you ever come back to, it's a dry year. Heck, we've just been through a desert and a fire. I reckon we can handle a bit of a dry stretch if it'll get us there faster. At the rate we're goin', I reckon that seventy miles could save us a solid week!"

"I ain't doin' it," Landon said flatly, and turned to walk back to his wagon.

"Well, you can do whatever ya like!" Marvin turned on him with unexpected rage. "Me, I'm headin' off that way soon as we hit that fork, and there ain't a thing you can do about it." He glared at Landon's departing back for a moment and then turned back to his captive audience. "Anyone who wants t' reach Oregon a week ahead of the rest of these suckers, you're more than welcome t' join me. We'll get first choice for the best land parcels, too. Try that on for size!"

Landon still made no response, and Noel knew why. He had observed Landon long enough to know that he said what needed to be said and then left folks to make up their own minds about what they were going to do with the information he had given them. It was a way of doing things that appealed to Noel, although he didn't think he possessed the skill set to make it a way of life for himself. Landon wore it like a well-tailored suit.

The nooning ended with a bit of a nervous buzz hovering over the camp. As the wagons rolled one by one onto the trail, Noel kept a watchful eye on the owners, trying to discover by their posture and gestures who were going to follow Marvin and who was going to stick with Landon. He knew his constant alertness would make the afternoon pass slowly, but there was nothing he could do about it.

A few hours into the afternoon, the fork in the trail came clearly into view. Landon's wagon was leading and rolled right on past it, as everyone surely had known it would. The Henderson's wagon followed along behind Landon's. Equally predictable.

Next was Marvin's rig with his uppity mules. With an extra loud, "Hup! Get up there!" to his draft animals, and a showy crack of the whip, he swung off onto the Sublette Cutoff.

One by one, the wagons passed. Noel stuck resolutely to following Landon's dust, but there were three other wagons besides Marvin's that left the main trail and struck out after the dissenter. One of them was Jack Grayson, no surprise, but when Mrs. Southey followed on after him, Noel felt regret lie shallow in his soul. Still, as Landon would have, he let those go who had made up their minds to follow the cutoff and silently wished them the best.

They had been only a day or two on the trail down to Fort Bridger when Noel noticed a strange-looking group up ahead of them on the trail. His wagon was leading, and he could see ahead down into the valley. There appeared to be only a few wagons drawn by oxen or mules. The rest were small handcarts pushed and pulled by men with their own two hands.

Noel blinked, feeling like he must be imagining things, but when he focused his eyes once more, they were still there, just as they had been before. Landon came riding back from scouting ahead, and Noel took the chance to ask him about them.

"No, you ain't seein' things," Landon told him. "Those are what folks call Mormons, and they're pullin' handcarts, all right. Mostly 'cause they're cheaper, and it saves 'em looking for water an' grazin', takin' care of hooves and shoes. Saves 'em harnessin' and unharnessin', too. Don't know that I'd want t' pull one of those things full of my family's goods all the way across the mountains, though."

Noel had to agree with him on that count, but there was a certain sense of admiration in his heart when they caught up to the Mormons and their handcarts at nooning time. There were at least a hundred of them, and more women than men, which was unusual especially out on the trail. Noel couldn't help stealing frequent glances at them.

"How'd you like t' mosey on over there with me an' hear what they're about," Landon's voice made Noel jump so hard that he almost upset his lunch onto the ground.

"Oh... I... sure," Noel stammered, rising quickly to his feet. He didn't know if Landon had asked because he saw him ogling the people or if he had another reason, but he would not pass up the chance.

The Mormons were cautious about letting them into their camp and elected instead to send out a representative.

"What do you want from us?" the man asked in a clipped and detached manner, surprising Noel.

They didn't look any different to regular folk, except for the fact they mostly used handcarts. Yet the friendliness he had expected from such industrious people was conspicuously lacking.

"It's a good evenin' to you, too," Landon greeted the man phlegmatically, ignoring his question that was clearly meant to discourage too much interaction.

"Yeah, let's keep it that way," the man snapped back, looking agitated. Noel was at a loss to understand what was going on.

"I ain't lookin' for trouble, if that's what you're thinkin'," Landon informed him calmly. "Matter of fact, I was hopin' you folks could help us bypass as much trouble as possible."

"I don't see how we can do that," the man snapped and seemed to ready himself to leave them and return to his kinfolk. He was stopped in his tracks when Landon kept on speaking as if the man had said nothing at all.

"See, we're down t' seven wagons from thirteen, and since we all know there's safety in numbers, I was hopin' we could stay close by y'all until we get to Fort Bridger, at least."

The man seemed taken aback. He floundered for a moment or two and then said shortly, "Do whatever you like," before turning on his heel and disappearing into the crowded campsite behind him.

Chapter 9
Cat and Mouse

Noel told the story of his and Landon's interesting interaction with the Mormons that evening at supper. "I ain't sure what could make a man so unfriendly," he commented as he finished recounting the conversation, "but I am sure we can't count on much help from them if things go south again with our little group."

"The Mormons have suffered a lot of persecution in their time," Anna remarked without a drop of chastisement in her voice, but Noel felt himself compelled to listen and learn.

"From what I heard, they brought it on themselves," Connor offered. "It doesn't seem Christian to have more than one wife."

"And to some, like us, it isn't. I don't believe it is biblical either," Anna replied. "The question is: are they doing harm?"

"Some say they are," Connor replied. "They shut themselves off, staying closed up in their own communities, and try to take over cities with their strange ideas about being some kind of a new nation of Israel to replace the old one."

"Is that the truth?" Anna asked simply.

Connor faltered. "It's what I've heard," he said, his voice careful. He seemed to be aware he was walking a tightrope, and any wrong answer could fatally trip him up.

"In situations like these, it's often difficult to tell where the first offence began. Besides which, I find it wholly unrealistic to lump all people sharing one characteristic into a whole of uniform sameness. If there are so many diverse elements among us, why would there not be the same among them?"

The faces around the fire were quiet and ruminative.

Noel contemplated Anna's words. "You mean we've tarred 'em all with the same brush and most likely they only keep to themselves 'cause they've been treated ill too many times before?" He was looking for understanding. For all his life, he had simply lashed out at what hadn't felt right. Either lashed out or run away. Now he wanted to see deeper. He wanted to see the things people like Landon and Anna saw.

"I couldn't have said it better myself, Noel," Anna agreed.

"I'll own I never thought of it that way," Connor confessed, tossing a chicken bone into the fire. "I just can't get used to the idea that they marry more than one wife."

"That's understandable," Anna conceded. "But what do you think will be more likely to turn them: censure and persecution or real and genuine conversations?"

A palpable silence hung over the shrunken group of emigrants while Anna's words echoed in their minds. Noel knew which one had the most lasting effect on himself, and he guessed it must be true for most people then, since he considered himself a rather average fellow.

They stayed with the Mormon group, with Landon taking the Mormon man's parting outburst as tacit consent to stay just a stone's throw away from the large group as they traveled the trail. A few curious children sometimes broke ranks to come and stare at their small group, and the four families' children sometimes tried to entice them into the wagon circle to play a game or show them something, but they only ever came within a few feet of the camp and then darted away, apparently afraid of the repercussions should their parents find out they were cavorting with the heathen Christians.

On the third night since the group had passed the Sublette Cutoff, Noel was sitting by the fire, softly playing his banjo. He hadn't been able to sleep, though he wasn't sure why. He hoped the music would help lull him into a self-induced sleep. At once, a voice beside him made him jump.

"Thought you could get away from me, did ya?" the voice said.

Noel wished he could have been mistaken, but he knew—without looking into the face of the man beside him—it was Fred Johnson.

"Mighty smart play, there, makin' me think you were with another wagon train. But lucky for me, there's pretty much only one trail to Oregon. Real sweet that. Makes my job a heck of a lot easier, even with a slippery customer like yourself, Mr. Tanner." Fred's tones were icy and his words calculated. He clearly didn't enjoy having rings run around him. Then again, who did?

"I told ya, for the umpteenth time, I'm good for it," Noel growled through clenched teeth.

"You can tell that to the jury when we haul you in front of the judge," Fred shot back. He got up and helped himself to a cup of coffee from the pot still hanging over the fire, which was by now barely more than a pile of smoldering coals. "Let's just get some things straight," he said in an affected matter-of-fact tone as he settled down again beside Noel. "Mr. Carlton knows where you are, and he didn't take kindly to your little trick of sellin' off your place to that Mr. Granville Taylor, especially since he's got some kind of clout. I ain't sure what."

Noel would have rejoiced at this bit of news if Fred wasn't sitting next to him, making him feel like he was about to reap all the wild oats he had sown in the last few months.

"Matter of fact," Fred continued with a little smirk, "Mr. Carlton's put out a warrant for your arrest. You're a wanted man in all the states and territories." The smirk became a grin, and a gold tooth twinkled dully in the faint light of the fire and the few lanterns dotted about the camp. "Put a price of three hundred dollars on your head, though I can't for the life of me figure out how you could be worth so much."

Noel's skin crawled. He had never thought about that possibility. Being a wanted man didn't feel as exhilarating as the penny dreadfuls made it sound. All he felt was fear. Fear for his safety, his family's safety, the safety of those who he was traveling with to the land of promise. If only Carlton would hold off till he could get back on his feet. "I reckon there ain't nothin' for it but to hand myself over then," he said grimly. "I ain't got the pony now, but like I've been tryin' t' tell ya all along, I'm good for it once I'm settled in Oregon."

Fred snorted. "You sure are a greenhorn, ain't ya?" he sniggered. "You really figure they won't chuck you in the clanger and leave ya t' rot there for a few years? Besides, you owe Mr. Carlton a heck of a lot more'n three hundred dollars. And I sure ain't givin' it all to him, anyhow, since I'm the one ran you down."

So that was it, Noel realized, his confidence waning by the second. They were squeezing him into a corner. Maybe if he just gave them what they wanted, they would leave him alone. "So what do ya want from me, then?" he asked flatly.

Fred grunted. "That's more like it, cowpoke," he said with a faint gloating in his voice. "You're a slow learner, but once you cotton on, you cotton on good."

Noel ignored the remark.

Fred leaned back expansively and began picking at his teeth with a grass straw. "I'm headed for the goldfields. California. And it ain't smart for a man t' go on his own and stake a claim. Feller with no kind of backup is a sittin' duck, askin' t' have himself fleeced. Otherwise, he's stuck there on his claim. Can't even go relieve himself without worryin' about someone stealin' from his lode while his back's turned."

Noel listened silently. He already knew where this was going. If someone had offered him the same thing earlier along the trail, he would probably have grabbed at the opportunity with both hands, but he knew something had changed inside of him across those long arduous, peril-fraught miles he and Dearbhla and their two little ones had just crossed.

"So here's what I'm suggestin'," Fred went on, clearly confident in Noel's imminent capitulation. "You come with me, an' we'll share a claim. Whatever we dig out, we split slap down the middle. When you make enough t' pay back Mr. Carlton what you owe him, you can light out, and I'll make sure those warrants get withdrawn."

He had called it a suggestion, but Noel knew it was nothing of the kind. Fred had just simply laid out the plans he had made for the next few months of Noel's life, and he really had no say in the matter. On the one hand, though, it would be a quicker way to get the money he needed and have Vernon Carlton off his back for good. "You'd best just stay clear of the wagon train," he said, without looking at Fred. "These folks ain't likely to let me go easy. Let me just stay with 'em until the split in the trail. I'll figure out how t' prepare them before we get there."

Fred gave a soft, knowing chuckle. "Just you remember, I'll be watchin' ya," he said in a low growl. Then he got up and sauntered off as if his being there was the most natural thing in the world.

Noel returned his banjo to its case and retired to his bed under the wagon. Early the next morning, the sound of the night watchman's rifle roused him, and he rolled over, groaning and covering his ears.

"Here, love, I've brought you a cuppa," Dearbhla's voice sounded beside him only moments later.

"You're up so early?" he asked groggily, rolling back to face her and reaching out to receive the welcome cup of steaming coffee.

"Aye. I couldn't sleep." Her face showed little, but Noel knew her well enough to know something was eating her.

"You heard me last night, didn't ya?" he asked after he had swallowed down his first sip.

Dearbhla sat down on the ground beside him and nodded.

"How much did ya hear?"

"I heard him say Carlton's got a warrant out for you, and I heard you agree to go with him once we reach the split in the trail."

Noel sighed. He had hoped he would have some time to figure out exactly how he was going to break it to her, much more gently than he and Fred had discussed it. But now the fat was in the fire, and he was going to have to deal with it. "They ain't left me with much of a choice. You see that, don't ya, Derv?" he asked pleadingly.

"And you're just goin' t' believe a skunk like Fred, who works—or worked—for an even bigger skunk like Vernon Carlton, that there's a price on your head?" She wasn't berating him, but her question went deep.

"Why would he lie about that?"

"To get you to do what he wants, of course," came the pragmatic reply. "If I were you, I'd call their bluff, Noel. If there really is a warrant with your name on it, let the law deal with it. He didn't show you any warrant, did he?"

Noel shook his head, but it tied his gut up in knots. "That there's just too big of a risk," he insisted. "It makes perfect sense Carlton would've done something like that. He's up to it, Lord knows."

"You have a newborn son and a little girl who need you, Noel," Dearbhla reminded him, her eyes pleading with him.

He knew she meant she needed him, too. Everything was just so uncertain. What was truth? What was lying? How could he possibly know? "Either way, there's a risk, ain't there?" he asked, shrugging. "He knows where I am, now." He paused and then corrected himself, "He knows where *we* are, now, and he'll come for us either way."

"You need to stand up to him, Noel," Dearbhla insisted. "You can't let him lead you around by the nose like this. He said he'd be watching us. I don't want that hanging over me along the rest of the trail. We're fewer now than we were before, and the Mormons will be gone soon, for what they're worth."

"What if I get arrested and thrown in jail?" he asked, wanting her to understand.

"How many sheriffs offices have you seen along the trail so far?" Dearbhla countered.

Noel had no response. She was right. As usual. His father had told him on his wedding day that a man's wife was the voice of truth in his life, and he would do well to take heed of what she said. It was the best advice his old man had ever given him, and he knew now would be a good time to follow it. "All right," he conceded. "I'll keep an eye out for Fred. He's liable t' be back sometime soon. I'll tell him the deal's off. Maybe if I write out a proper IOU and have him sign a copy, that'll help smooth things over with the law, if'n when I ever run into 'em."

Dearbhla leaned over and gave him a peck on the cheek. "You're a good man, Noel Tanner," she praised him warmly. "Breakfast will be ready soon. Best get yourself washed up."

The gray morning was just beginning to show a tint of orange in the sky and the camp was already a hive of activity as Noel stumbled off to the Green River to wash. The Tanners, Slades, Hendersons, and Morlands enjoyed an almost carefree breakfast, and then the wagon train rolled out slowly back onto the trail.

Noel walked alongside the oxen, one eye constantly scanning the horizon for any sign of Vernon's lackey, but two days rolled by before he glimpsed the man again. He had carefully written out a rather formal declaration of debt owed, in duplicate, and provided a space for both himself and Fred, as Vernon Carlton's representative, to sign as a sign that both had agreed to the terms.

He didn't say so to Dearbhla, but he wondered if it was possible Fred would sign the IOU. He remembered Dearbhla telling him he would have to stand up to the man and call his bluff. He quaked a little in his boots. Both Vernon and Fred were intimidating men. Neither of them seemed to have an ounce of compassion, not even in the nail of their little toe.

It was while they were passing a ridge to their right that he spotted the man on horseback watching them from above. It was surely Fred, and he was making good on his word to keep an eye on Noel.

"Derv," Noel said, stepping closer to her as she rode along on Jasper. "I need the horse. Fred's on the ridge."

Dearbhla snapped to attention, casting a quick glance up at the ridge. "Where's the IOU?"

"In the saddlebag."

Dearbhla handed a protesting Fiona to her father and slid down from the saddle. Tristan still rested peacefully in the makeshift sling she had gotten into the habit of carrying him in across her chest to free up her hands.

"Take Landon with you," she urged Noel as he stepped hastily into the leathers.

"There ain't time," Noel responded, eager to get the negotiations over and done with.

He galloped off before Dearbhla could say another word. He knew Fred would watch and most likely guessing that he was on his way to him.

He let Jasper's reins hang loose when they reached the base of the ridge, and the sure-footed horse picked his way effortlessly up the side of the incline. At the top, Noel looked back. The wagon train had become small in the distance, crawling along like a strange, disconnected sidewinder, moving across the semi-desert floor.

Looking back to the front, he cast around to glimpse Fred and eventually spotted him riding away toward the creek on the other side of the ridge. Nudging Jasper's sides, Noel urged the horse into a canter. When he reached Fred, the man didn't look too happy to see him.

"What's your game, cowpoke?" Fred asked irritably. "You ain't supposed t' draw attention t' me like that."

"I changed my mind," Noel replied, coming straight to the point. "I got an IOU here for you an' me both t' sign in duplicate. I'm good on my word. You can tell Carlton I'm awful sorry for what I did, sneakin' off an' all, but I seen the error of my ways, and I'll make good on what I owe soon as I can."

"I ain't signin' no IOU!" Fred snarled. "You're comin' with me to the goldfields, and that's it. There ain't no other way out of it, boy."

Both of their horses were feeling the tension mounting in the air and they started snorting and shying.

"I'm sorry, Fred. I ain't doin' what you ask. I know I agreed earlier, but I've seen sense, and there ain't no way I can leave my family out here in the wilderness to go chasin' after gold."

Without warning, Fred drew his revolver, leveling it at Noel. "You'll come with me, or I'll put a lead pill in your gut," he snarled.

Noel froze. He had never been quick on the draw. Any move he made for his own revolver now would be fatal. For him, not Fred. He tried as best he could to settle the nervous horse prancing beneath him.

"You'll come with me right now, or I shoot you between the eyes," Fred threatened again, pulling back the hammer.

A shot rang out, and Jasper snorted, arching his back like a bronc and giving a little leap to the side. Noel saw Fred twist sideways as a red stain appeared on his gun arm. Fred's hand swung up, and the gun discharged. Noel gripped the pommel horn with both hands to keep from falling off and dropped low along the horse's neck just as he heard the zing of a bullet whizzing past his ear.

Dear God in heaven, he thought. *Help me get out of this alive, and I'll do anything You ask. I swear it. Anything at all.*

Chapter 10
Fort Bridger

With an oath, Fred holstered his pistol and kicked his horse's sides aggressively. The animal sprang away, carrying him off into the distance over the treeless land. Noel regained control of Jasper and was about to set off in pursuit when a voice cried out behind him.

"You stay right where you are, Noel Tanner!"

It was the unmistakably authoritative tone of Landon Morland.

Noel turned Jasper around and watched Landon riding closer. Suddenly, the crimson on Fred's shirt made sense. "You fired at him?" Noel asked.

"I hit his gun arm on purpose, if that's what you're askin'," Landon informed him dryly. "That was a dang fool thing you did, Tanner," he added, his eyes narrowing. "You're lucky your wife told me you were off after an outlaw without backup, else you'd be lyin' in a gully with the life leakin' out of you right now."

Noel hung his head in shame. He knew Landon was right. There were no excuses to be made. "What about Johnson?" he asked. "He'll be back, no doubt about it."

"Sure, but at least for now you're breathin'. An' while you are, you better tell me what all this is about. I don't take to it kindly, you bringin' danger on the wagon train. As I recall, we've had this conversation before."

Noel nodded silently, still not able to bring himself to make eye contact. The tough old cowhand was no walkover and even less of a fool. Not that Noel had ever thought he was, but it brought home to him the sobering realization that he would have to think more than twice before he went off half-cocked like that again.

While the two rode back to the wagon train, Noel told Landon the entire story. The seasoned trail man allowed Noel to complete his narration without interruption.

"And now I ain't sure which way t' turn. They ain't givin' me another option. It's the goldfields or the noose, pretty much," he concluded despondently.

"Or Fred's bullet," Landon reminded him.

"Or that," Noel agreed.

"Well, the way I see it, we ain't got much choice as a group, either, except t' hang tight together an' keep this coyote off our heels, just until can get to Fort Bridger. I know there ain't dragoons there anymore. Army abandoned the place a while back, but hopefully we'll find some kind of help for this peck of trouble you're in."

Landon called a meeting at their next stop and the men of the camp all agreed. They would rally around Noel and his family and push hard to reach Fort Bridger as soon as they could. Noel felt the guilt and shame wash over him as it became clear how much trouble his single, fool-headed decision back in Independence had brought on the good people around him.

And here they were, giving him their support when they might just as well have left him to sort out his own troubles. He resolved once again that he would do everything humanly possible not to make his problems their problems anymore. After all, he had brought them on himself.

For the next five days, the pioneers pressed on, keeping the wagons as close together as they could. Everyone had their eye on the horizon, but all they spotted were a few mule deer and a coyote or two, peering down at them curiously from the higher ground. At last they made it to the fort, and the overlanders breathed a collective sigh of relief as they circled the wagons outside the rather dilapidated huddle of adobe buildings that comprised Fort Bridger.

Landon wasted no time. With the sun still hovering midway in the afternoon sky, he fetched Noel from his wagon, leaving Clyde, Connor, Brady, and Matt with strict instructions to take care of Dearbhla and her children.

"We're goin' t' see who's in charge, and we're goin' t' have a little talk with 'em," he stated simply as he steered Noel from the camp by the arm. After some enquiries made to the local cowboys lounging about the fort, they located the man who ran it.

Horace Beecher was a stocky man who stomped around with an air of superiority mingled with a strange combination of magnanimity and pity. His blond hair was covered by an ancient bowler hat that seemed to have been pierced through by either an arrow or a bullet. It also sported more than a few dents. His wide grin showed off a gold tooth among his rows of yellowed gnashers. He chewed incessantly on a wad of tobacco and smelled of whiskey.

"Welcome, folks! Welcome!" he boomed as they entered his dingy office that seemed to double as his living quarters. "I hope you'll find Fort Bridger has everything you need! Be sure an' holler if you're short on anything, now, y'hear? Anything at all!"

Landon nodded slowly. "Thank you kindly, Mr. Beecher," he said. "Matter of fact, we're needin' some assistance, if you'd be willin' and able t' help?"

Beecher snapped to immediate attention. "Willin' I am. Able, I can't vouch for until I've heard what it is y'all need, but heck, I'll give it my best shot, fellers." He grinned, opening his arms wide.

"My friend here is havin' a little trouble with a feller from his past, and we were hopin' you could point us to the law in this area," Landon explained.

"The law?" Beecher gave them a sidelong look. "Ain't such a thing here. It's every man for himself and the devil take the rest, if y'all get my meanin'. But I might be able t' figure somethin' out for ya. Care t' tell me some more?"

"Yes," Noel blurted out. "There's a man goes by the name of Fred Johnson. He's been houndin' me, an' he's got t' be stopped. Won't take an IOU. He's fixin' t' kill me or kidnap me." He told Beecher a short version of his story.

"Whoa! Steady on there, cowboy!" Beecher exclaimed, raising his hands as if in surrender. "That's a mighty long list of grievances you got there "

"They're all the truth," Noel insisted, frowning slightly. He had been hoping for some kind of help from this man, but he seemed too light in the breeches to care about much other than being the lord of his ramshackle little castle.

"Well," Beecher replied, folding his arms over his chest. "If that's the way things are, I reckon I'll be a poor neighbor if I don't help y'all out as best I can." He leaned forward, pressing his fingertips together and showing them all his teeth. "You fellers give me till mornin', and I'll see what I can do."

Noel regarded him dubiously for a moment, then decided he didn't know the man well enough to be able to make any accurate judgments about him. "All right," he agreed, nodding grimly. "We'll give ya till mornin'."

Noel left Horace Beecher's office feeling more than a little uneasy. He could tell Landon felt the same way. Still, there was nothing for it but to wait.

***

Horace waited until the pioneers and locals were all drunk or asleep before he ventured out from his adobe house and skirted the large Mormon camp. The man he was looking for had pitched a tent near the Shoshone village that had recently established itself a little way off from the old fort. He found him roasting some buffalo meat over a small fire in front of his temporary sleeping quarters. The stranger had intrigued Horace. He seemed like a loner, as Horace himself was, and he had looked a little down in the mouth about something. Now Horace knew what it was.

"Howdy, stranger!" he greeted as he neared the man's camp. It wasn't wise to jump in front of a man without announcing oneself. More than one fool uneducated in the ways of the wild west had met his untimely end that way.

"Howdy yourself," grumbled the man.

"I couldn't help noticin' your getup," Horace went on, unfazed by the man's apparent desire to be left alone. "You headed down to the goldfields, ain't ya?"

"And what if I am?" came the gruff reply.

"You fixin' t' take along a feller, goes by the handle of Noel Tanner?"

The man's head shot up, his beady eyes searching Horace's face. "Can't say I've heard that name before," he lied, not fooling Horace in the least.

He had dealt with many travelers coming through his little trading post and most had their little secrets they were wearing on their sleeves. "Well, he sure has heard yours," Horace replied, making himself comfortable by the man's fire. "Matter of fact, sounds to me like he's seen too much of ya."

"That ain't any business of yours, mister," the man groused, cutting a piece off his buffalo meat and checking to see if it was cooked yet.

"Now, see, that's where you're wrong," Horace said in a perfectly matter-of-fact tone. "I just made it my business. Anythin' goin' on in my tradin' post, that's my business."

"Well I reckon I'll just move on out," the man snarled back, his eyes glinting in the firelight.

"You could, but then you might have yourself a little accident, traveling in the night and all. Everybody knows it ain't the safest time t' travel, 'specially a man by his lonesome."

"What's your beef with me, mister," the man shot back, clearly irritated.

Horace laughed. "Beef? I ain't got a beef with ya. I'm just here t' help. You give me that warrant, and I'll take care of our little friend Tanner."

"Warrant?" the man sneered. "Now, see here, I can only give a feller something that actually exists."

Horace nodded, understanding slowly filling his mind. He was sensing that something connected him and Fred Johnson by more than just their solitariness. "I hear ya," he said. "Give a man a little motivation, and he'll do anything for ya, right?"

Johnson nodded, slicing another piece of buffalo meat off the stick.

"Problem is, that feller's got too many folks lookin' out for him. You've got to take a more subtle approach," Horace continued.

Johnson paused in his chewing. "You tryin' t' tell me how t' do my business?" he growled.

"Just giving a little advice, based on years of experience," Horace replied blithely. "The way I see it, the warrant wasn't a bad idea, but you need t' set him more at ease. Make him think you're helpin' him, not the other way around."

"All right, Mr. Know-it-all," Johnson said, still sounding irritable. "Why don't ya tell us *your* fantastic plan."

Horace didn't need a second invitation. "I'll tell the boy I met up with some dragoons and they told me the best would be for him t' go with ya. Don't you worry yourself about a thing, I'll take care of everything. All I want is a cut of the gold you fellers dig out."

Johnson eyed him skeptically. "You'll handle the boy and his crowd?" he asked. "You'll soft soap 'em t' let him go?"

"Quicker'n you can say mother lode," Horace assured his reluctant partner in crime.

The gears were clearly turning in Fred Johnson's head.

Horace waited patiently. He knew when he had his man. There was no need for any more convincing.

Johnson cut another slice off the roasting meat on the stick and offered it to Horace, who took it with a smile. "You got yourself a deal," Johnson said, still looking skeptical but a little amused, as if he expected Horace to fail and looked forward to watching the spectacle.

"Good," Horace replied, ignoring his new partner's facial expressions. "I told him and his guardian t' come back in the mornin' and I'd tell them what I managed t' sniff out. Expect me when ya see me, but don't light a shuck out o' here before that happens, y'hear?"

Johnson grunted his assent, and Horace felt his work was done. A nice little extra income would come his way soon, and he welcomed it with deep gratification.

***

The next morning, the pioneers darkened his doorway as he had asked them to do, and he ushered them gravely into his office. Declining the coffee he offered them, they sat opposite him on the two rickety wooden chairs he set out for them.

Taking his place behind his desk, he pressed his fingers together in front of his chin and breathed a great sigh for effect. "I'm afraid it ain't good news I have for ya this mornin', young man," he said with a well-practiced melancholy air. "I ran into some dragoons last night, and we had ourselves some mighty enlightenin' conversation, if I'm honest."

Noel and his guardian, a tall, sharp-eyed man dressed like a cowhand, glanced at each other in concern. He waited until their attention was back on him before he continued.

"We all agree it ain't fair of your creditors t' demand what you ain't got to give 'em, but that warrant ain't goin' away by itself. Best thing you can do is just pony up soon as you can. Would be a dang shame t' see ya coolin' yer heels in the clanger while your poor missus and kids had t' fend for themselves out there in Oregon."

He paused, waiting for that awful truth to sink in before he offered the lifeline.

"Now, I'll also agree with ya that Fred Johnson feller, well, he ain't got the knowhow of dealin' with folks. Feller like that is real ham-fisted and rubs everyone up the wrong way. But the truth of it is, he can't take no IOU back to his boss. He'd be fired right off, no questions asked. You got t' see things from his side, too."

The younger man was clearly taking in every word, and Horace could smell success coming closer with every word. The older man's expression was inscrutable, which was a little upsetting to Horace. He wasn't used to not being able to read people. Still, he kept his composure and continued.

"I spoke with him last night, y'see. What them dragoons said is true. He ain't got much of a choice. Now, maybe he didn't do things right, but I showed him the error of his ways, an' he's agreed t' go easy on ya. Where I can help ya is I can give ya both contacts in California, folks who know where the real paydirt is. They'll get y'all in where you can make a lot of money in a short time and be done with this millstone round yer neck."

The older man, who had introduced himself as Landon, interjected, "So you're sayin' Noel's got no choice but t' do as Johnson says?"

Horace nodded grimly. "Looks that way, mister," he confirmed with melancholy gravity.

Landon shook his head firmly. "We can't let him do that." He rose as if to leave, but Noel gripped his wrist.

"Landon, I've been enough trouble to the kind folks of the wagon train already. Maybe this is my way out. Mr. Beecher here is tellin' the truth. There's no other way out of this. I know you and the others will take good care of my Dearbhla and my babies. You got t' let me fix my own shenanigans, or they'll never go away."

Horace inwardly rubbed his hands together with glee. It was working. Better than he had expected. The Tanner fellow was as naïve as he looked, and his guardian seemed like one of those straight-laced fools who let others make their own decisions. Horace had learned early in life that most people didn't know what was good for them and needed to be helped into the right decisions most of the time. He was more than willing to fill that role, always had been. He watched the Landon fellow's face with interest. Just as he had expected, the older man capitulated.

"I ain't tellin' ya what to do, Noel," he said, his voice sounding a little tired. "Like you said, it's your shenanigans, and you got t' fix it the best way you can. I'm jus' sayin', I reckon you'd be better off with us. Them goldfields ain't all they're cracked up t' be."

"Maybe so," Noel conceded, and Horace held his breath. "But I have Mr. Beecher here t' send me in the right direction. Maybe this is what's supposed t' happen. Maybe this is providence, givin' me a way out."

Landon shrugged, and Horace silently let out his pent up air, trying not to smile too broadly. "I think you're makin' a wise choice, young feller," he said as sagely as he knew how.

Landon's eyes narrowed, but he said nothing.

***

"Noel, please!" Dearbhla begged him that night as he laid out his plan to her. "You can't go with that weasel! We spoke about this already!"

"I know, Derv," Noel replied, trying to soothe her distress. "It ain't an easy decision t' make, but I've made it, and I have t' see it through. I've been runnin' too long, and the more I run, the more I'm puttin' y'all in danger. You, the kids, the other overlanders. Heck, these people have done me more good than I deserve, an' all I do is bring trouble on 'em. It's the only way we can be free of Vernon Carlton, honey, don't ya see that?"

"I wish I could believe that this plan of yours will even work," Dearbhla mourned.

"Don't ya have faith in me?" Noel felt a little stab of injury to his pride as a man.

"Faith? I have faith in *you*, Noel. I know you'll do the best you can by anyone and everyone. It's Johnson I don't trust. Nor this Beecher feller. How do we know he's not pullin' the wool over our eyes, too?"

"We don't, Derv, but that's the chance we'll have t' take."

Dearbhla was silent for a while. "It's still a few day's travel before we hit the split in the trail," she whispered. "I'll keep hoping you change your mind."

Noel didn't tell her he was hoping the same thing. He knew his mind was made up, and he didn't want to give her or himself any false hope.

Chapter 11
Soda Springs

The following twelve days of travel were stressful ones for Dearbhla. It didn't help, either, that she had been feeling weaker and weaker since Tristan's birth, but she didn't want to bother Noel with any complaints about that.

"Your da already has so much on his plate, we'd best not add any more troubles to it," she whispered softly to the sleeping babe huddled in the crude hammock around her neck.

She had stitched it a little, so she didn't need to fold and tie it every time, and it had attracted the admiration of some of the other women in the camp. Jasper stumbled over a large stone on the trail, and Tristan woke. His clear blue eyes gazed up trustingly into hers, and she smiled at him.

"Sorry to wake you, my little shamrock," she said, blowing him a kiss.

Tristan's baby face broke into a toothless grin, his little eyes twinkling as he cooed at her.

Dearbhla laughed. "Right on time, little man!" she exclaimed. "Fiona started giving me grins like that when she was your age, too."

Tristan cooed again, kicking his feet against his hammock and shaking his little fists with obvious glee, as if he understood what she had said. A spell of dizziness overcame her suddenly, and she had to hold on to the pommel horn to stop herself from falling off.

Thankfully, Fiona was with the Slades, spending time with her best friend, the Slades' silent and reserved little boy, Gabor. Dearbhla peered into the distance and wondered how long it was before nooning. The heat shimmered over the trail. Even though it was not the searing oven they had experienced on the east side of the Great Divide, it seemed to Dearbhla that it was too much for her failing strength to handle.

"You all right, love?" Noel's worried voice startled her.

She looked down to see him walking beside Jasper, his hand on the horse's rein. "Just feeling a little dizzy," she reassured him, smiling down with what she hoped was a cheerful expression. "I think it must be the heat."

"It ain't all that hot, this side of the mountain," he said, the worry increasing instead of going away as she had hoped it would.

"Perhaps I'm just tired," she insisted, refusing to admit that she was, in fact, utterly exhausted and wanted to just lie down and sleep for days on end.

"You can ride in the wagon, if you'd like," Noel suggested.

"You know as well as I do, that's not a good idea. These oxen have to last until Oregon. We can't overload them."

"I'd rather have you lastin' 'til Oregon than the oxen," Noel reminded her.

"That's why I love you, Noel Tanner," she replied, her heart warming toward him. She found herself suddenly in a quandary. She had been wishing the miles away, but now the awful truth loomed up in her mind that the further they went, the closer they were to the fork in the road that led to the California goldfields. Instinctively, she glanced around, looking for a glimpse of Fred Johnson.

She had been tense for most of the past twelve days, casting frequent glances to the hills and ridges that rose up around them. Noel had said nothing, but she had caught him doing the same more times than she could remember. She looked down at him again, and the look on his face made her want to climb down off the horse right there and hug him.

"You're feeling guilty, Noel. I can see it. You need to stop beating yourself over the head for everything. We all make mistakes. Heaven knows, I've needed you to take the brunt of some of mine. We'll get through this. Together. The way we get through everything."

Noel's face crumpled a little, and he turned his head away. Just then, the sound of galloping hooves arrested their attention.

Matt came galloping along the train on the scraggly horse he and Brady had found when they rescued Carrie. "We're almost at Soda Springs!" he called out jubilantly, his face wreathed with smiles.

"Soda Springs? What on earth is that?" Dearbhla asked.

"They call it the oasis of the Oregon Trail,'" Noel informed her, the smile back on his face as he looked up at her. "Landon told us all about it last night when you were already dreaming in the wagon. I'll let ya see for yourself."

Her curiosity for the moment distracting her from her tired and aching limbs, Dearbhla sat up straight in the saddle and scanned the horizon for some kind of water feature. It was not long before she saw what her husband was referring to.

A great swath of white earth, looking almost like a mirror, was spread out along the mountainside. All around it were rocks of brilliant orange, deep red, and rich yellow, and many strange cone-shaped formations. Steam rose from various places, and here and there, little spurts of frothing water jets rose into the air at irregular intervals.

Beyond the cluster of strange pools was a wide, blue river carving its way through the mountains. Juniper, pitch pine, and cedar trees displaying stunted growth were scattered across the unusual landscape, but beyond the river to the west, rich forests blanketed the mountainside in luxuriant greenery.

Dearbhla stared oper-mouthed in amazement. There seemed to be quite a few people dotted about, and she could see circled wagon trains and small booths set up where people clustered, apparently sampling some wares.

As soon as her group had circled their own wagons, she begged Noel to take her and the children to see the shimmering pools. He agreed, and soon the family was picking their way among the cauldrons of bubbling water. Some were hot to the touch, almost to the point of scalding them. Others were more tepid, but most of them smelled of sulfur.

The ones that got the most attention were those that bubbled with gas trapped inside the water, like the soda water Dearbhla had seen in the shops in Independence. She had never really acquired a taste for it, but here it seemed to be a sought-after delicacy, at least if one was to go by the crowds of travelers swarming around the booths that Dearbhla and Noel discovered to be selling the naturally carbonated water in bottles. Some with strong entrepreneurial spirits had even added different flavorings and espoused the rejuvenating properties of their particular brew.

"Maybe you should try some of those for your tiredness," Noel suggested gently.

Dearbhla shook her head. The smell of the sulfur was making her nauseous. Instead, she contented herself with roaming around the cone fields that were dotted with tufts of grass, some of which hid more pools.

While they were walking around one particularly large pool, gently bubbling away with no outlet and not seeming to increase or reduce its water content, Dearbhla stepped a little too far to the side. The next moment, she slipped into the tepid waters.

She gasped, immediately lifting Tristan up in her hands. "Oh! Heavens above! Noel!" she cried, imagining herself and her son disappearing into the bowels of the earth. Thankfully, the pool was far less deep than it was wide, and she sat waist deep in the water.

Tristan stared at her, wide-eyed, while Fiona giggled. Noel, apparently trying very hard to control himself, let a little chuckle loose and then swallowed it. But Dearbhla felt herself relax and instead of clambering out in a fit of embarrassment, she simply sat in the warm water and laughed, holding her son in the air. Soon the entire family was laughing heartily until Noel could compose himself enough to take Tristan from her outstretched arms.

"Hold on a second, honey," he told her. "I'll just find a safe place to put this little feller down, then I'll help you out."

"No, please, I'd like to stay in here a little longer," Dearbhla said to Noel's obvious surprise. "It's really very pleasant. I feel as if the effervescence of the water is doing something good." She shifted a little lower into the water until it was almost up to her chin.

"Well, all right," Noel agreed, looking a little hesitant. "You know, the trappers around here swear high and low they get drunk on this water. I hope you ain't goin' t' get drunk, too."

Dearbhla laughed. "I'm lying in it, you great oaf! Not drinking it!"

Noel winked at her as he hung Tristan's hammock around his neck and found a rock to sit on, trying hard to dissuade Fiona from jumping in beside her mother. At last, he spotted a smaller cauldron nearby, and with Dearbhla's laughing permission, he let the little girl do her own soaking in a bubbling pool. She quickly got bored with that pursuit though, and soon she was leading Noel in a merry dance around the rest of the area, comparing pool sizes and rock colors and water temperatures.

Dearbhla closed her eyes and let the warm, mineral waters do their magic on her aching muscles. She hardly knew how much time had passed, but when Noel came to fetch her, she noticed the sun was almost touching the mountain peaks on the western horizon.

That evening, back in camp, dried off and feeling better than she had in a long time, she begged Landon to let them stay for another day, as they had at Independence Rock.

Landon looked around the circle of faces lining the firepit, seeming to draw from each one's facial expression what they thought of Dearbhla's request. "Well, since tomorrow is the Sabbath, I reckon we could spare a day for rest. As I recall, Anna was askin' not too long ago if we could rest for a day at least every other Sunday, an' give those who wish t' observe the holy day a chance t' do that."

Dearbhla smiled gratefully. "Thank you, Landon. And Anna," she said.

Once again, Noel jumped in and took care of most of the chores that needed to be done the next day. Fiona entertained the Slades and Anna took care of baby Tristan, while Dearbhla spent many hours soaking in the strangely rejuvenating waters of the effervescent pool she had stumbled into the day before.

A passing stranger advised her to alternate between soaking in the warm waters and dipping in the cooler waters of the Bear River afterward. It was then that she made the discovery of the Steamboat Spring. A larger sulfur spring that spouted out from the banks of the river and made a loud hissing and roaring sound like the steamboats that traveled up and down the Missouri River.

Whether it was the pool itself or a combination of the warm and cold waters mixed with hours of sweet rest and Anna's heartfelt Sunday message, she could not tell, but the evening of the Sabbath day found her more full of life than she had been since Tristan's birth.

Despite the happy respite, her gut still twisted at the thought of Noel going off to California with Fred Johnson while she continued on to Oregon with their not-so-new friends. Every night, she prayed he would change his mind and stay with the group. She knew Noel well enough to know talking would do no good. Besides, if she managed to talk him out of it, she feared he might resent her for it later.

***

Two days after they left Soda Springs, the little caravan reached the place where the California trail broke away from the main trail and headed southwest. Noel spotted Fred waiting by the side of the trail long before they reached him, and this time, the henchman wasn't shy to show his face.

"Ready t' go, Tanner?" he asked flatly, his face expressionless as Noel turned aside from the trail to speak to him.

"Just let us circle the wagons for noonin', then I'll join ya," he negotiated, feeling his heart sinking. He really didn't want to go, but the vow he had made not to cause any more trouble for the wagon train weighed heavily on his conscience.

"Hurry up about it, then," Johnson agreed reluctantly, and Noel returned to Dearbhla's side.

"I'm sorry I have to take Jasper," he apologized to his wife as he packed the saddle bags with pemmican, hardtack, and some dried beans and rice for when he cooked.

"After Soda Springs, I'm feeling much stronger, don't you worry. And maybe the boys will catch a wild mustang for us, like they've been promising for the last month." Dearbhla smiled bravely, trying to keep their farewell light. He loved her for it, and it actually made it even more difficult for him to leave.

"I promise I'll ride straight up t' Willamette Valley, soon as I've made enough to pay Vernon and wired him the dough." He fastened the strap on the saddle bag and turned to take her in his arms. "You know what? Maybe I'll even make a little more so we can buy us some really good breedin' cattle an' start a winnin' herd. That way we'll get even richer, even quicker, and you'll never have t' worry about any Fred Johnsons knockin' on our door ever again."

For a moment, she kept silent. Then she said softly, "I'd rather have a hundred Fred Johnsons knocking on my door as long as I knew you were in the house with me."

Noel felt his heart break. "I will be, sooner than you think. I promise, Derv." Noel's voice was cracking, and he knew he had to leave immediately or he might change his mind on the spot. He kissed his wife and baby son and twirled Fiona up in the air. "Papa's goin' away for a bit, sweetheart," he said. "You be a brave girl and take care of Mam and Tris, now, y'hear. I'll see you sooner than ya think."

"I will, Papa," she said, planting a kiss on his cheek.

Noel rode away with frequent backward glances at his family. When he couldn't see them anymore, he looked ahead to the trail and saw Fred Johnson waiting impatiently a few feet along the California trail. Silently, he rode up to him, and the man turned his horse's head without a word. It was only that evening, when they stopped for the night, that the silence was broken.

"You mind if I see that warrant?" Noel asked Johnson.

For a moment of awkward silence, he received no reply, and then the henchman answered brusquely, "You think I'd keep that on me?"

"Not even a poster?" Noel enquired. "I'd just like t' see it for myself. Heck, I ain't ever had a warrant against me. I'm kind of curious to see how the poster looks. See if they got my likeness right, you know?"

"Oh, it looks like you, all right," Johnson replied snarkily. "Ugly as heck. Says, 'Wanted for thievin', four hundred dollar reward.'"

Noel looked up from the coffee he was nursing. "Four hundred? I could have sworn ya said three hundred before."

"Three hundred, four hundred, what's the difference?" Fred snarled and rose to his feet. "I'm goin' t' hit the sack, an' I'd advise ya t' do the same. We got a lot of miles t' cover tomorrow."

Noel wondered why he hadn't thought of asking Fred to show him the warrant earlier. It seemed, in that moment, to be the most logical thing to do, and yet he had simply believed it when Vernon's henchman had told him he was a wanted man. Even Dearbhla, not someone who could be expected to be well versed in the ways of treacherous men, had questioned whether Fred was telling the truth or making up stories.

Add to that the fact Fred had named a different bounty price each time, and there was a strong case for suspicion building in Noel's mind. Still, neither of those factors conclusively proved there was no warrant against his name. The only way he could find out that for sure was to find a sheriff's office somewhere. If they had communicated the warrant to all the territories, as Fred had claimed, someone at a sheriff's office would have a record of it.

And there ain't much chance of that happenin' before we get closer to the diggin', Noel thought dismally. Salt Lake City was the only place nearby that could have a sheriff's office, and that was in the opposite direction from the way they were going. Noel turned in for the night and hardly slept a wink. The whole next day he spent trying to figure out how he could escape, but nothing foolproof came to mind.

The tree covering was sparse, with mainly small piñon pine and winter-fat shrubs, offering little opportunity for a hiding place, and he already knew Fred likely had a much faster gun hand than he did. By the evening of the second day, he had all but given up. Deciding to wait until they reached the towns near the heart of the goldfields, he resigned himself to many days of missing his family.

But when they stopped at noontime to rest and water their horses at a creek, a party of riders came by, stopping a little way downriver. Fred was asleep under a box elder with his hat over his face, so Noel took a chance to sneak closer and see who had crossed his path.

"Hello, the camp!" he called out as he neared them, holding his gun hand high in the air.

The men all turned to look at him. One of them stood up, a tall man with a pitch-black mustache. "Howdy, stranger. You alone out here?"

"No, sir, my friend's catchin' some shut-eye back there, and it didn't feel right to wake a tired man from his beauty sleep." Noel was making things up as he went along, but his mind was not as much focused on what he was saying as it was on what he saw in front of him. There, in the noonday's light, a silver, star-shaped badge glinted on the lanky man's chest.

Chapter 12
Reversed Roles

"Anything we can do for ya, mister?" one of the other men asked, but Noel hardly heard him.

"You're a sheriff?" he asked the tall man.

"I reckon so, since I'm wearin' the badge. Me and my two deputies here, we're trackin' some horse thieves. You fellers seen anything?"

Noel shook his head. "No, no, sir," he said, his head spinning.

"Well, if y'all do, you can tell 'em Sheriff Redford is lookin' for 'em, so they'd better grow eyes in the back of their heads."

Noel nodded as the men turned away, and then his tongue seemed to come loose from its frozen state. "Sir, Sheriff Redford," he blurted out, stepping forward boldly to the middle of the group. "My name's Noel Tanner, from Independence, Missouri." His heart was beating wildly in his chest. If he was wrong, and Vernon had actually put out a warrant for his arrest, they would recognize his name in an instant, and he would be behind bars in a couple of days.

"Well," the sheriff said slowly as he turned to eye Noel with a wary expression, "we're mighty pleased t' make your acquaintance, Noel Tanner." He looked to his deputies, his face mirroring their expressions of confusion.

"You havin' some kind of trouble, Tanner?" one deputy asked.

Noel paused. He had to make sure they didn't recognize his name before he could spell out to them the trouble he was in. "I was wonderin' if my name rang any bells for y'all," he replied cryptically after a moment's hesitation.

The three men looked at each other again, their confusion compounded. All three shook their heads, and the sheriff turned to face Noel. "You mind tellin' us what all these peculiar statements are about?"

Noel took a deep breath. "Feller told me there was a warrant for my arrest sent to all the territories. See, I took off on the Oregon Trail, leavin' a lot of unpaid debt behind, and this feller worked for the feller I owe." He felt his face grow hot as he admitted his foolishness to the upstanding lawmen before him.

"Well, if there is a warrant with your name on it, we ain't heard of it," Sheriff Redman said slowly. Then he turned to his deputies. "You fellers remember a name like that?"

The two deputies shook their heads, still looking a little confused.

"I know it ain't a regular thing for a feller to ask, but I need t' know if it's a lie," Noel tried to help them understand. "You didn't get a wanted poster with my face on it? With a three or four hundred dollar reward offered?"

The two deputies burst out laughing.

The sheriff kept a straight face, but it was clear his sobriety resulted from a gargantuan effort. "Now, listen here, sonny," he breathed, as one might speak to a person who wasn't fully in command of their faculties. "I reckon you've been had. There ain't a sheriff's office in God's green earth is goin' t' post a reward that big for a feller who didn't pony up for his debt. And we know the names on our list of wanted felons better than we know our own names. Yours ain't one of 'em."

Noel felt a moment of shame wash over him for even believing Fred Johnson's stories, but there was an even greater emotion filling him. It was anger. Anger that the man had badgered him and lied to him, anger that he had been bamboozled so easily, anger that he was two full days' ride from the people who cared for him most in all the world.

Ignoring the sniggers of mirth still erupting from the deputies, Noel stood up straight. "Thank you, sir, for that information. Seein' as I'm a free man, I'll be leavin' right away. I got a family back on the Oregon Trail who needs me."

As he completed his sentence, the two deputies sobered up, a strange look on their faces, as if they were recognizing someone. But they weren't looking at him.

Noel spun around to see Fred marching straight toward him. "Tanner, what in tarnation you think you're doin', sneakin' off like that while I'm sleepin'?" he shouted, apparently not paying much attention to the other men behind Noel.

"Well, seein' as I ain't a wanted felon, I figure I can do what I like without your say-so or anyone else's, Fred Johnson," Noel retorted, starting off toward their camp and his waiting horse. As he passed Johnson, he spat on the ground at his kidnapper's feet.

"What's the meanin' of this?" Johnson demanded, grabbing at Noel's arm and spinning him round to face him.

Noel glared at him. "There ain't a warrant, is there, Johnson? And no reward, neither. You made it all up jus' to get me to play your little game."

"So what if I did?" Johnson sneered. "You're miles away from anyone who can help you now, and you'll do what I say if you want to see your precious family again."

"Your game's up, Johnson. You can't scare me anymore," Noel snarled, jerking his arm loose and resuming his furious storming back to his horse.

"Don't you take another step, Tanner!" Johnson yelled.

But Noel kept on walking. Not even the sound of the hammer being pulled back on the henchman's gun could make him slow his pace.

"I'm warnin' ya!" Johnson's voice rang out again, but he may as well have said nothing at all at the rate Noel kept moving. Noel knew the man needed him alive. He was no use to Fred as a dead man. For once, he was going to call Johnson's bluff.

The next few seconds happened so fast that, afterward, Noel had trouble remembering exactly what had happened when. As best he recalled, the first thing he felt was a searing pain rip through his shoulder. In that exact moment, he spun around, reaching for his revolver. Lifting it, he pointed right at Fred Johnson and pulled the trigger, but all he heard was an empty, resounding click.

Johnson was raising his gun once more, taking aim and pulling back the hammer.

Breaking out in a cold sweat, Noel cocked the gun and pulled the trigger again. Once more, the hollow click of the hammer hitting home reached his ears, but this time there was another sound, too. The rapport of three gunshots echoed off the surrounding hills, and Johnson's body jerked. His revolver fell to the ground with a dull thud, and he sank to his knees with a bewildered look on his face, his eyes glazing over. Then he pitched forward slowly, face-first into the dirt, and lay still.

Noel felt his knees turn to jelly. He stared at the three men on the other side of Johnson's lifeless body. They looked back at him as calmly as they had when they first saw him calling out to their camp.

"Fred Johnson. Now that's a name we *do* recognize," Sheriff Redman said, holstering his firearm. "Murdered an old man for his horse an' sold it to another poor sod who was none the wiser."

Noel couldn't find any words to reply.

"This the feller who was tellin' you you're a wanted man?" one deputy asked, stepping forward and rolling the body over with his boot to see for himself whether Johnson was actually dead.

"Yeah," Noel replied, finding his voice again.

"Figures," the sheriff remarked dryly. "He got a horse?"

"A dapple gray with black legs," Noel replied mechanically, still trying to process the fact that he was not a wanted man and Fred Johnson was dead. Never mind the fact that Johnson himself had been the wanted man, all the while making him think it was him the law was after.

"Alright, that one was actually his own horse. I reckon you can take it as a reward for bringin' us a wanted man. That horse'll fetch ya about a hundred dollars at one of those forts along the trail."

"Wild prices they make the poor suckers pay for supplies along the trail. Milkin' folk who are already pretty dry. It don't seem right," the deputy remarked, but Noel hardly heard him.

"So I can go now?" he asked, feeling nauseated and wanting to get away. Back to Dearbhla and their precious children. Back to the safety and sanity of his friends, Landon and Clyde and Connor, and their families.

"Sure you can," the sheriff assured him. "You're a free man, ain't ya?"

Noel managed a weak smile and then turned on his heel and almost ran back to the camp, where Jasper waited patiently. Quickly packing everything into the saddle bags, he mounted up and tied the dapple gray's reins to the pommel horn of his own saddle. As he rode off, headed back along the trail Johnson had led him along, he spoke to Jasper's pricked ears.

"That sidewinder emptied my Colt," he said, hardly believing the words coming out of his own mouth. "No wonder he didn't make me give it to him." Noel tried to remember when Fred could have done it, but concluded it must have been during the night while he was sleeping. How he hadn't noticed the difference in weight he also didn't understand. All he could put it down to was the fact he had been wound tight as a spring on a clock.

He shuddered when he considered how close he had come to death. With an empty barrel on his Colt, he had been a dead man walking. The way Johnson had thoroughly fooled him made him feel ashamed and angry, but he marveled at the ingenuity of the man, now dead.

It sure was brilliant, he thought to himself as he rode along the creek, following the trail. *What easier way to keep a feller from running to the law or lookin' for help? Anybody who thinks he's a wanted man is goin' t' hide his face no matter where he goes. It's like he was puttin' his own guilt on me.*

The thought was sobering. Mostly because Noel had so readily accepted that guilt. He had so readily believed he was the worst kind of man and taken on every lie that Johnson had dished up to him. He knew he was learning something, and it was not an easy lesson, but he was a different man now. A man who would not run from his mistakes or his problems anymore.

For the rest of the day, he rode hard, stubbornly ignoring the pain in his shoulder. When night fell, he stopped, mainly to rest the horses, get some food down his gullet, and fill his water canteens. Then he inspected the wound. A clear entry and exit hole were visible in the front and back of the flesh just above his clavicle. The bullet seemed to have missed the bone by a fraction of an inch, from what he could tell.

He washed off the bloodstains and cleaned up the wound as best he could, and then lay down and fell into a brief, restless sleep that lasted only for a couple of hours. He woke with a start, dreaming of Dearbhla calling for him to come back, and saddled up the two horses again. This time, he put his saddle on the dapple gray to give Jasper a rest from carrying the weight of a man on his back.

Riding through the night, Noel ignored his body's calls for sleep, hoping he wouldn't run into anybody else on the trail. He had as much as he could take from thieving, heartless men who gave no thought to anyone but themselves. Thankfully, the trail Fred had chosen was a less traveled one, for reasons that were now abundantly obvious to Noel.

A few hours before dawn, he stopped again to rest and eat. Then he hit the trail once more, knowing that soon he would reach the main Oregon Trail. Once he did, it was much easier going, and he rode the horses alternately, letting them settle into that easy, loping canter that only mustangs seemed to possess and could carry them across miles of wilderness without stopping. He passed a couple of wagon trains, a few hunting parties, and even a traveling Shoshone village.

It was already late in the day by the time he saw the whitewashed adobe buildings of Fort Hall. This fort really looked like a fort. High walls encircled it, topped with a guard tower at two corners and smoking chimney stacks along one wall. Around it were the usual encampments of emigrants' wagons, dragoons' tents, and Shoshone villages, although all were fewer than the crowds that had gathered around either Fort Kearney or Fort Laramie.

The brutality of the trail was surely taking its toll and weeding out those who had come along either ill prepared or lacking in strength and character. Or both. Noel knew now that if he wanted to survive the rest of the trail to Oregon, he had better pay better attention to how he approached the rest of the journey. As he rode through the rabble of humanity surrounding the fort, he searched for a familiar face, listening for familiar voices.

"Papa! Papa!" a shrill cry rose above the babble of campside noise, and tears immediately sprang to Noel's eyes. He would have recognized little Fiona's voice anywhere. She came running to him from a circle of wagons, waving her skinny arms in the air, her fiery red curls flying in the wind.

Noel dismounted and strode toward her. As his little girl reached him, he fell to his knees and embraced her, crying shamelessly. Moments later, he felt Dearbhla's arms embracing them both and sobs shook his body. "I'm so sorry. I'm so sorry," was all he could say, repeatedly.

At last, Dearbhla drew back and helped him to his feet while Fiona clung to his hand, stroking it concernedly and saying, "It's okay, Papa. Don't cry, Papa," while she looked up into his face with an earnest expression in her innocent eyes.

"Yes, my angel," he replied, smiling through his tears. "I know it's okay. I'm crying because I'm so happy to see you."

"Happy crying?" she asked, looking even more perplexed.

Noel laughed. "One day when you're all grown up, you'll understand, don't you worry, my little honey flapjack!"

His lifted mood seemed to convince her of things his words couldn't, and she relaxed visibly, swinging his hand in hers. "We got an extra horse, Papa?" she asked, gazing up at the dapple gray walking beside Noel.

"Yes, we did. Papa helped a sheriff stop a terrible man, and so he gave us the wicked man's horse." He turned his attention to Dearbhla. Her cheeks were streaked with tears, too, and her eyes were full of questions he knew she was holding back with difficulty.

"Won't the wicked man come looking for his horse?" she asked.

"No, he won't. The sheriff and his deputies bedded him down on Boot Hill," Noel euphemized to protect his little girl's thoughts.

Dearbhla led him to the fire, where he was greeted with many careful hugs and slaps on the back. Everybody seemed to understand that questions should not be asked until their prodigal member had filled his belly, had his wound tended to by Anna's capable hands, and had a good night's rest for the first time in three days.

Chapter 13
Birds of a Feather

Noel woke to shrill cries of anger and protestation. His head still hurt, and he felt groggy, but there was no way he could sleep a minute longer with that racket carrying on. Besides, it appeared to be well after sunrise if the light shining through the tent canvas was anything to go by.

He crawled out on all fours, his wounded shoulder feeling stiff and painful, and peered into the glaring sunlight. People he didn't know were standing around making angry gestures and all talking at once. One of them, a big, burly man with a bushy red beard, was hanging onto little Billy Henderson's arm. The boy's face was stricken with guilt and fear. Noel knew that look all too well. Almost as well as he knew the emotions that caused it.

He struggled from the tent just as Clyde Henderson stepped into the circle of wagons and retrieved his son from the enraged stranger's grasp. Noel moved closer, trying to ignore the throbbing in his head.

"Who's going to tell me what in the world is going on here?" Clyde demanded in his quiet but adamant way. He didn't instill fear in people the way Landon did, but he had a calm authority about him that made a man understand he would not lie down and let anyone walk all over him.

"This thievin' little rat stole from us," the redheaded man claimed stridently, jabbing a forefinger into Billy's shoulder as he spoke. Billy retreated against his father's protective bulk.

"Stole what?" Clyde placed his arms protectively over his son's shoulders.

"My prize chickens," the man spat. "An' I want 'em back."

"Did you steal this man's chickens, Billy?" Clyde asked his son in a matter-of-fact tone.

"No, Pa, but..." the boy replied.

"Don't lie, you little coyote!" the man interrupted him roughly. "I'll wager we'll find 'em right here in this camp if you give us a chance t' look around," the man said, folding his arms.

"All I've got is your word. You can't seriously expect me to allow you to nose around our wagons just because you claim my boy stole your chickens." Clyde put his foot down. "If you don't have any proof of my son stealing from you, then you've no cause to come accusing him and demanding anything from us."

"Pa," Billy said, "I got t' tell ya somethin'."

Clyde shook his head, hushing up his boy. "We'll talk later," he said. Turning his gaze back on the crowd gathered, he told them, "Until you can provide proof, I'll thank you to leave me and my family alone."

He placed his hands on Billy's shoulders and steered him firmly away from the angry group. Landon had also arrived in the meantime and quickly handled the red-bearded man and his crowd of fellow accusers. As they were sent away, gesturing and protesting, Noel noticed a boy of about the same age as Billy hovering around the outskirts of the group and snickering quietly to himself.

As the group left and Clyde led his son away, the boy caught Billy's eye and pulled a face at him. Billy scowled, but offered no other action in return. Noel wondered what that nonverbal communication was all about and did a little investigating on his own. Grabbing the items for his ablutions, he headed off to the nearby creek, watching the crowd of Billy's accusers to see which camp they returned to.

It was a slightly larger camp than their own, comprising ten wagons to their seven. The boy who had pulled a face at Billy scampered up to a prairie schooner, where an old man sat stuffing what looked like fluffy, pure white feathers into a pillow he was making. The boy looked rather pleased with himself and began chatting amicably with the old man.

Noel ducked down to the creek, where he washed and dressed behind a chokecherry bush. The water was cool and refreshing. He felt his headache give way slightly, but not fully leave him in peace. Still, at least he could think a little straighter, and that was all he needed to do now, for Billy's sake.

The families had already finished breakfast, having left him to sleep off his arduous little adventure and most were now taking care of laundry, repairing whatever needed repairing on their wagons, and cooking good solid meals of meat, vegetables, and all the trappings that there was usually no time for on the trail itself. Many of the men had gone off to get supplies and were most likely absorbed in haggling with the merchants to bring down their astronomical prices.

Noel sat down on the wagon tongue to enjoy the breakfast Dearbhla had set aside for him before she had left, possibly to take care of their laundry down at the river. As he chewed, he considered selling the gray horse, but quickly decided against it. An animal like that could come in handy as they progressed along the trail. It was clearly a tough, hardy mustang. Just the kind they would need in the unforgiving mountains that lay ahead on their trail.

For a while, Noel pottered about, fixing what he could on the wagon, greasing the wheels and checking that the steel wheels were all still firmly attached, tightening the screws that had shaken loose. Once he had satisfied himself, there was nothing more to be done, he took a stroll around the fort and see if he could find out anything helpful about Billy's little antagonist.

Sauntering past the boy's camp, he spotted the youngster lashing an empty chicken coop to the underside of a wagon. "You folks already ate up all your chickens?" he asked with mock horror in his voice. "How're you goin' t' eat dry bacon without eggs for the rest of the trip? You know it's over eight weeks t' go, right?"

The boy looked up, at first ready to defend himself, and then he saw the clownish look on Noel's face. His own face split into a cautious grin. "They'll sure taste good for noon meal, though," the boy shot back.

Noel let out a loud guffaw. "How many chickens you plannin' on shovin' down your pie hole, young feller?" he asked jokingly.

"Oh, don't fret yourself, mister," the boy returned, clearly relaxing and enjoying the banter with the strange grown-up. "I sold most of 'em."

"That's good business sense," Noel replied, feigning seriousness and pulling a dour face.

The boy laughed. "'Specially when you didn't raise most of 'em yourself an' they didn't cost you a penny."

"Now you're talkin'," Noel replied, taking mental note of the boy's words. "One hundred percent profit ain't any kind of loss, now, is it?"

"No, sir, it's not," the boy replied, looking chuffed with himself.

"Except to the poor sucker who raised 'em," Noel continued in a stage whisper. "Best thing you can do is sell him the feathers in a pillow, and he won't even know he's buyin' back his own chickens."

"Or sell 'em to him in a pie!" The boy hooted with laughter and gripped his sides. "You sure are funny, mister," he added, wiping his eyes.

"And you sure are smart," Noel flattered him. He sidled closer. "You ain't lookin' for a business partner now, are ya?"

"Maybe I am, maybe I ain't," the boy replied cryptically, crossing his arms over his chest but still clearly enjoying the interaction. "My business is pretty sensitive, if you know what I mean. Can't have just anyone I don't know gettin' in on it."

"Even smarter than I thought," Noel flattered him some more. "I bet the feller you fleeced for them chickens thinks some other poor sod helped himself and you're walkin' away unscathed, eh?"

The boy glanced around, looking a little unsure for a moment if he should continue to open his mouth quite so wide about his dealings. "You're pretty smart yourself, mister," he said. "Maybe you and me *could* be partners, like you said."

"I tell ya what," Noel replied. "Why don't ya come over to my camp at noon time and we'll talk on it some more?"

"Sure," the boy agreed.

"An' bring along those pillows your ol' man was stuffin' earlier. Reckon I might have a buyer for ya," Noel concluded, and they shook on it.

Noel wasted no time after that. He quickly sought out the red-bearded man and found him haggling over fox pelts with some Shoshone men. Waiting patiently until the bartering was over, he greeted the bearded man and introduced himself.

"Mighty pleased t' meet ya, Mr. Tanner," Harvey Gould said, looking a little irritated at the stranger trying to make his acquaintance. "There a reason you're botherin' me?"

"There sure is, Mr. Gould," Noel replied expansively. "And I think you'd like t' hear it."

"Would I now?" Gould began walking back toward his camp, the pelts slung over his arm.

"It's about them chickens you had stolen. I reckon I can prove who stole 'em." Noel hoped his plan was going to work. For Billy's sake, he had to make it work.

Gould stopped abruptly and looked at Noel. "I already know who stole 'em. Charlie told me."

"Sure he did, but the way I hear it, the little feller's pa is askin' for proof, and you ain't got any," Noel reminded him.

"How do you know all this," Gould asked suspiciously.

"I get around," Noel replied with a conspiratorial wink.

Gould contemplated his new acquaintance's words for a moment. "All right," he agreed. "Show me what ya got."

"Oh, I ain't got the proof with me. It'll only work if ya meet me at the thief's camp at noonin' time," Noel told him. "You do that, and the boy's father will have to pony up for what his son took."

Gould resumed walking. "I'll be there, Tanner," he said over his shoulder. "An' you'd better not be playin' me for a fool if you know what's good for ya."

Noel watched him go and then darted over to the wagon trail. He found Billy under his family's wagon, listlessly whittling away at a stick with his pocketknife. "Billy," Noel said, scooching in beside the boy, "I need ya t' tell me everything about Charlie and the chickens."

Billy stopped whittling and stared at Noel, wide-eyed. "You know Charlie?"

"Let's just say him an' me, we had us a little chat a while back," Noel responded with a smile. "He had some mighty interesting things t' say."

Billy's face fell. "He caught me out good, Mr. Tanner," he lamented sorrowfully.

"And how'd he do that, Billy boy?" Noel prodded.

"Well, me and Charlie were playin', you know, spittin' competitions, sword fightin' with sticks, that sort of thing. Next thing he says, 'Let's pull a prank on someone.'"

Billy paused, looking around to see if anyone was listening. Satisfied they were properly alone, he continued.

"Then he takes me over to Mr. Gould's wagon and unhooks the chicken coop. 'We'll just hide 'em away for a bit, shake him up a little, for a joke,' he says, and so we carry the chickens over to the bushes and hide 'em there. We went back to playing, and I swear I clean forgot about 'em."

Noel nodded, clear understanding breaking through like sunlight on a cloudy day. "You remember if there was anything special about those chickens?"

"Yeah," Billy nodded sadly. "I remember Mr. Gould said they were a special breed he wanted t' make a lot of money out of in Oregon. They were whiter than snow, and they looked fluffy. I ain't seen chickens like that before. When Mr. Gould started looking for 'em, he got real mad, *real* mad, Mr. Tanner. Charlie told me tc go get them, but when I did, they were gone." His face crumpled with fear and remorse.

Noel encircled the boy's shoulder with one arm and gave him a comforting squeeze.

"Charlie told Mr. Gould it was me that took 'em and showed him where we'd hid 'em. Mr. Gould was threatenin' me and yellin' so loud. It was so scary. I know I shouldn't have played along with Charlie. I thought it was just for fun. I didn't think the chickens would get stolen."

"You ain't to blame for those chickens gettin' stolen, y'hear?" Noel assured the sniffing youngster. "Today at noon time, we'll sort it all out. You an' me. You'll see, it'll all work out fine and dandy."

Billy lifted his freckled, tear-streaked face, hopelessness etched in his eyes. "Only you and my pa will believe me, Mr. Tanner. The rest of the folks think 'cause I like to play pranks, that means I'm a thief. But it ain't true. It just ain't true!"

"I know, half-pint." Noel used Landon's nickname for the boy. "You're goin' t' have t' trust me, y'hear?" He couldn't help thinking how he and young Billy really were birds of a feather.

Billy sniffled. "Okay, Mr. Tanner," he said, more obediently than with any kind of relief evident in his voice.

Noon rolled around soon enough, and the families in the camp gathered around their pit fires for their communal midday meal. Noel winked at Billy from where he sat beside Dearbhla. The boy gave him a wan smile and continued picking at his stew and dumplings.

They had barely finished eating when Noel noticed young Charlie peeping at him from behind the Morland's wagon. "Hello there, young Charlie!" he called out, purposely giving away the boy's presence. "Why don't you come join us for a spell?"

Charlie reluctantly emerged and skulked over to where Noel sat, holding the two pillows on his lap. Billy's face turned white and then red. He gave Noel a questioning look. Noel nodded encouragingly, conscious that Billy would rather have been a million miles from there if he had to go by the way the boy was squirming in his seat.

As if on cue, moments later, he heard the gruff bass tones of Harvey Gould behind him. "I'm lookin' for a feller, name of Noel Tanner," he announced. "Anybody seen 'im round here?"

Noel stood up and turned to face Gould. "Right over here, Mr. Gould. Why don't ya take a seat here with us?"

"You said you had proof of who stole my chickens," Gould growled. "I ain't here for socializin'."

"I figured," Noel assured him. "If you'll humor me, I'll get right to the point quicker'n you can say chicken pie."

As he uttered the last two words, Charlie gave a little jump beside him as if something had bitten him. Gould stepped into the circle and took the seat offered by Landon.

Noel remained standing. He cleared his throat. "Mr. Gould," he began his speech, "you say you had some chickens stolen this mornin', yeah?"

Gould nodded grimly.

"And you say young Charlie here told you it was our Billy who did it, is that right?"

"It is," Gould confirmed.

Charlie squirmed as if he knew he was in for something.

"I'm curious, Mr. Gould, did you buy some chicken pie for the noon meal from our friend Charlie?" Noel asked in the same tone of voice as before.

Gould looked at him quizzically. "Sure, I did, what's wrong with that?"

"Not a thing, nothin' at all," Noel assured him. "Did Charlie have any chickens of his own that he could make pie with, Mr. Gould?"

"Not far as I know," Gould replied slowly, stroking his beard. "Just a couple of scrawny wild chickens he caught in a trap. I figured I was helpin' him and his grandpa out..." His voice trailed off while Charlie's face grew redder by the second.

Noel turned to the boy. "Why don't you show us those new pillows of yours, Charlie?" he suggested mildly. Charlie scowled. "Mind tellin' us what kind of feathers you used t' stuff 'em?" He reached out to take one, but Charlie snatched it away angrily.

He stood to his feet, his eyes brimming with tears of fury, his bottom lip quivering ever so slightly. "I knew I shouldn't have trusted ya, mister," he spat.

"You got a problem tellin' us what's in those pillows, boy?" Gould asked him, suspicion clear in his face.

"Why don't ya find out for yerself!" Charlie yelled, hurling the offending pillows into the fire pit before he turned and fled the company gathered around the fire.

Noel sprang forward, plucking the pillows from the coals and dousing the smoldering cotton in the dirt. He turned them over and easily ripped the burned fabric open to reveal pristine white fluffy feathers inside. Billy gasped. Gould aired his lungs with an oath as he stood to his feet.

"You could have just told me, Tanner," he growled.

"Yeah, I reckon," Noel agreed, tilting his head to one side. "But would you have believed me, Mr. Gould?"

Gould mumbled something and removed himself from the group.

"Oh, I'm sorry, Mr. Gould, was that an apology to Billy for accusin' him of something he didn't do on the word of another child?" Noel asked, keeping his voice cool.

Gould stopped and looked down at the disbelieving Billy.

The young boy jumped to his feet. "No, it's me who should say sorry," Billy insisted. "I helped Charlie hide your chickens in the bushes, Mr. Gould, but I promise I thought it was just a prank. Honest to goodness, sir. That ain't a lie. I figured we'd put 'em back after you saw they were gone, but when I went to fetch 'em, they were gone, like they vanished into thin air."

"A prank, eh?" Gould muttered.

"Yes, sir," the boy said, hanging his head in shame. "I know it still ain't right. I'm sorry, sir."

Gould regarded him for a moment. "You didn't cook 'em, and you didn't stuff pillows with 'em, so I reckon my trouble ain't with you. Don't fret yourself about it, sonny boy." He turned to leave and then looked back. "And next time, just speak up, will ya? If you ain't the guilty party, ain't no reason you should pay the price for the felony."

Chapter 14
The Prodigal

A moment of stunned silence fell on the families seated in a circle. Some stared at Billy and some at Noel.

"I declare I feel as if my eyes and my ears have just deceived me," Anna said breathlessly, breaking the silence at last.

"Well, they haven't, love," Clyde assured her, rising from his seat and crossing over to where Noel still stood, feeling suddenly awkward. The older man reached for him and took his hand, shaking it firmly. "And we owe this young man a great debt of gratitude for clearing our son's name."

Noel wanted to look down, but the humble gratitude in the eyes of the man before him prevented him from doing so. "I figured I'd want someone to do that for little Tristan one day if he ever got caught up in a tight spot like that," he said. "You know what they say, boys will be boys."

"As hard as we try to make them into the little angels we ain't ever been, anyway," Landon added, stepping up beside Clyde and wringing Noel's other hand while he slapped him on the shoulder for good measure.

Noel laughed shyly. "That's exactly right, Landon," he agreed.

Anna appeared beside her husband with young Billy in tow. The boy's eyes were glistening with tears. "My son says he'd like to thank you for what you did for him, Noel," Anna said, pulling Billy around to stand in front of her and placing her hands on both his shoulders.

Noel hunkered down so he could be closer to Billy's eye level and waited patiently for him to speak.

"Thank you, Mr. Tanner," Billy said, his voice hoarse. "I ain't had no one besides my family do somethin' like that for me. Playin' that prank on Mr. Gould in the first place was wrong, but you still helped me. I'll never forget that. Never." Fat round tears spilled over his lashes and dropped to the dusty earth.

"Pardners look out for each other, didn't you know?" Noel said cheerfully. "Darn it, if I've learned anything on this trip so far, it's that."

Billy gave him a watery smile and wiped his eyes. "You learned that on this trip?" he asked incredulously.

"Sure I did, half-pint," Noel confirmed, taking off his hat and nodding vigorously. "I seen the way your pappy and Mr. Morland and Connor and young Matt and Brady. They just cover for a feller wherever he's lackin' and without expectin' a thing in return." He rose to his full height again, feeling as if he was about to burst into tears along with the boy in front of him. "Whatever I've done here today, it's because they did it for me first," he said, looking from Landon to Clyde and back again. "I don't know if it's repayment enough, but I'll do it again in a heartbeat, long as there's breath in my body."

"I never doubted you, Tanner," Landon said, his voice a little gruffer than usual.

That evening around the campfire, after the air had ceased trembling with Dearbhla's angel tones lifted in a couple of rousing shanties and a sweet lullaby, the friends reclined in the glow of the dying embers, enjoying the final moments of their last rest day before they braved the final, most treacherous part of their journey to the land of promise called Oregon.

"Noel," Brady said out of the blue. "You never told us what happened out there on the California trail."

"I learned my lesson is what happened," Noel responded cryptically.

"And I hope you'll do nothing like it again," Dearbhla said, sitting down beside him on the log he was occupying and leaning her head on his shoulder.

Noel felt his gut twist with shame. But just as quickly as it had come, he shook it off. No more was he going to carry the burden. As long as he learned from his mistakes, something good could come out of something that seemed all bad. "I sure won't," he said, placing an arm around his wife and pulling her closer. "Not if I can help it. First off, I reckon I'll be payin' more attention to what you've got to say about a thing before I go off makin' my own decisions. Truth is, I'm more hotheaded than what's good for my health. You were right after all, honey. I'm man enough to admit to that."

"Tell us about the Johnson feller," Brady prodded, apparently keen on a real-life drama story before he retired for the night.

"Johnson," Noel echoed reflectively. "He was a wily old coot, but not wily enough not to trip himself up. He figured he had me in the bag, except he was tightening the noose around his own neck."

"How so?" Brady asked.

"There was no warrant on my head, but there sure was one on his. Only I wouldn't have known it if I hadn't run into a sheriff and his posse out tracking down some horse thieves. Heaven only knows how they came to be noonin' at the same creek where we were, and on the same day at that."

"I think heaven had more to do with it than you'd imagine," Anna said, a soft smile gracing her face.

Noel didn't respond. He hadn't felt like he had any claims to make on heaven for a long time. It seemed unlikely he had any favors coming to him from that quarter. And yet he couldn't deny that it was wildly coincidental that the men who had facilitated his freedom would be in that exact spot at that exact time.

If he and Johnson had been further down the trail, who knows how long it might have taken him to get back to the wagon train and his family again? He would certainly not have been around to come to Billy's aid and clear the boy's name. In fact, it had all worked out so well, they would forgive one for believing that it was planned.

"One thing I know for sure," Noel said, looking around the group. "I'd be a dang fool to ever get shot of you folks. Me and Derv, we've kind of kept to ourselves most of the time, so we ain't seen the way community works. But you folks, you sure showed us what lookin' out for your neighbor means. You were here, takin' care of the three people who mean the most to me in all the world while I was runnin' around makin' wrong choices all over the place." He looked down at Dearbhla's hands wrapped in his. "If y'all will have us, I'd like for us to be neighbors forever."

Connor laughed. "Look who's gettin' all sentimental on us," he quipped.

"We'd be honored to have you as our neighbor, Noel," Louise said warmly.

"You're welcome to build your cabin next to mine any day of the week," Clyde chimed in.

Noel remembered a Bible story his mother had read to him once. Or maybe more than once. It was about a prodigal son who returned to his father after going well and truly by the wayside. Instead of demanding restitution for his son's sins, the father had welcomed him home, happy he was still alive and had come back to his family.

I reckon I got a tiny idea how that prodigal feller must have felt, Noel thought to himself. It was a feeling he had never experienced before. On the one hand, he never wanted to experience it again. On the other, he wished he could hold on to it forever.

The End

I would appreciate a positive review on Amazon.

More Classic Westerns are in the works...coming soon.